My big chance . . .

Dear **D**iary:

Tonight I went up to ask Mom if I could have a slumber party. I just know this party is my big chance to get into the cool crowd.

"I was just kind of thinking," I said to her, "that I'd like to have a slumber party."

"You mean have Nancy sleep over?"

"Well, sure, Nancy. But a few other girls, too. I don't know. Maybe Samantha and Candace."

"I thought you hated Samantha with a passion," Mom said.

"Well, I do. But I'm hating her less lately."

"Well, I suppose if you're dying to do this," she said.

"Oh, Mom!" I shouted, leaping up and giving her a big hug.

"Now wait just one more second," she said. "I want to see good grades on your next report card, or there aren't going to be *any* parties around here."

"Oh," I said.

"Is that going to be a problem?" she asked, looking suspicious. I hadn't mentioned the troubles I was having in history.

"Oh, no. No problem. No problem at all."

Dear Diary #1: *The Party*

Dear Diary #2: *The Secret*

Dear Diary #3: *The Dance*

SCHOLASTIC INC.
New York Toronto London Auckland Sydney

THE PARTY

Carrie Randall

AN
APPLE
PAPERBACK

SCHOLASTIC INC.
New York Toronto London Auckland Sydney

ISBN 0-590-42476-9

12 11 10 9 8 7 6 5 4 3 2 1   9/8 0 1 2 3 4/9

Printed in the U.S.A.   11

First Scholastic printing, August 1989

KEEP OUT!!
(This means you!)

This diary is the property
of

Elizabeth
Jane
Miletti

ALL TRESPASSERS WILL BE
PROSECUTED!

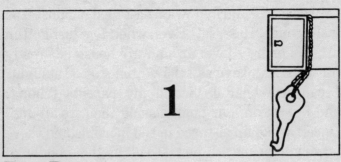

1

Dear **D**iary:

I can't believe I have you. And I really can't believe that I — Lizzie Miletti, definitely a non-writing type of eleven-year-old — am keeping a diary. Until today I'd never even thought of it. When I woke up this morning, it was the farthest thing from my mind.

Of course, *everything* was the farthest thing from my mind when I woke up this morning. I had punched my alarm clock off while I was really still asleep, and then put the pillow over my head, and missed the first twenty minutes of my day. A big day — my first one in sixth grade.

When I finally did wake up, I had to rush around like the Mad Hatter, trying to get myself together in ten minutes. Plus, my brother Josh was hogging the bathroom as usual, getting himself gorgeous (sixteen for a boy seems to be a terrible age) and my mom was downstairs using the other bathtub to give our cats — Marilyn Monroe and Elvis — a flea dip. Elvis was leaping out of the tub, going

3

"Mwaaack!" Marilyn was flattened against the wall, going "Hssssss!" Even when I've just gotten up, the energy level around my house is already full-blast. And even after I've gone to bed at night, I can still hear Josh and my parents talking, and Sebastian, our dog, chasing the cats around. Once I woke up at three in the morning and there wasn't a sound. I just stood in the middle of my room listening to the silence. It was almost weird.

When I couldn't get into either of our bathrooms, I ran up to my gram's apartment in the attic. In an emergency she lets me use her shower. That's because I am her favorite grandchild. She has never told me this in so many words. I just know.

Then I ran back down to my room to blow my hair dry. Luckily, I had my great first-day-of-school outfit laid out neatly on my desk chair. New black skirt, white turtleneck, and green cotton sweater. Green is my best color — it matches my eyes. All I had to do was dress and get out of the house. The getting out isn't always so easy.

For instance, just as I was about to go, my eight-year-old sister, Darcy, came in.

"Do the trees moving make the wind blow, or is it the other way around?" she asked like it was absolutely crucial that we get this settled right then and there. She can come up with the weirdest

4

questions, and she won't let you go until you've told her the answer. Sometimes I am very patient with Darcy. Other times, like this morning, I just put her off.

"We'll talk about it this afternoon," I told her, hoping she'd forget it by then. But she won't. Then I rushed down to the kitchen to pick up a stray piece of toast on my way out.

My dad and my thirteen-year-old brother, Adam, were sitting in the breakfast nook with Rose, whom everyone still calls "the baby," even though she's four. I could tell Dad was trying out some new product from his company — Roth Frozen Foods. He always tests the new food items out on us. Some of these, like milkshake waffles, are great, but with a lot of them it's easy to see why they are not going to make it onto any supermarket shelves. I could tell from the smell in the kitchen as I sailed through that this one was a doozy.

"Oh, honey," my dad called out when I was nearly out the back door. "Could you just try one of these?" He held out a plate with this Thing on it. It looked like a squashed, fried hockey puck.

I gave my brother Adam a question mark look, and he silently shook his head at me, as if to say — *don't.*

"Toaster clam roll," Dad said enthusiastically. Rose sat happily propped on two phone books,

5

eating one. Rose would eat anything. Josh calls her the Human Garbage Disposal.

"Mmmmm," I said. "It really looks great, but I'm late for school. It's our first day back. I want to make a good impression. You know."

But my dad wasn't so easily fooled.

"I'm afraid, Lizzie, that your Research and Development potential is sadly slipping. Not to mention your sense of adventure."

"Forget it, Dad," Adam said, looking up from the sports page of the newspaper, "you're just not going to get anyone, except the Human Garbage Disposal, to eat those grease globs."

Dad looked at the plate of clam rolls and nodded real thoughtfully. Then he said, "Maybe it's that America hasn't really gotten into clams as a breakfast food yet."

"Right, Dad," I said as I slipped out the door, into the backyard.

I thought about riding my bike to school, then decided against it. It would get me there faster, but it was hard to look sophisticated on a bike. I figured, I'm in sixth grade this year, the top grade in the school. I have my image to think of now. None of the cool girls in my class rides a bike anymore. Unfortunately my best friend, Nancy Underpeace, was waiting at the corner — and she'd decided to ride her bike. She was standing there with it leaning against her side.

"I thought we were going to ride to school together," she said.

"I forgot," I fibbed. "I'll just walk alongside you."

In addition to being my *best* friend, Nancy Underpeace is also my *oldest* friend. We've known each other since we were born. We've always looked like the Odd Couple, though. I am petite (some people would just call it short, I guess), and Nancy has been the tallest girl in our class every year since first grade.

We would gladly trade heights with each other. Actually, there are a *few* trades we'd gladly make with each other. One is our hair. I hate my frizz. Whenever the humidity goes up, I look like I'm wearing a brillo hat. Nancy thinks this looks wild and funky. "Like Cher," she told me once, then thought about it a little more and added, "Well, like Cher would look if she were short and eleven years old." Anyway, Nancy would love to trade her hair for mine. She considers hers boringly straight, although to me it seems perfect — thick and blonde.

Another trade we'd make is names. I hate my first name. It's short for Elizabeth, and I wish people would call me Beth, or Liza, or something — anything but Lizzie. Nancy hates her last name — Underpeace. After five years of grade school with kids calling her everything from Underpants to Undertaker to Underwater, she would — more than anything in the world — like to be a Smith.

As we walked along together, I noticed Nancy hadn't made any attempt at all to look sharp for the first day of school. She had on an old Smurfs sweatshirt her grandmother had sent her ages ago, and some jeans that looked like she'd been climbing trees in them. Sometimes Nancy still acts like she's about seven years old. Until this summer, the two of us have always been peas in a pod, thoughtwise, but lately I've begun to feel quite a bit older than her. More mature, if you know what I mean.

"Oh, I need to get a notebook," she said, when we were almost to school, walking by the little shopping center on Spruce Street. She wanted to get a spiral notebook at MacDermott's stationery store.

While she was inside, I was just kind of hanging out, looking in the window. Most of the stuff there was pretty boring. You know, the usual — staplers, boxes of typing paper. But then, suddenly, there in the middle of the other things, I saw you, Diary. I thought, oh how cute and old-fashioned looking, with that ivory-colored leather cover and little brass clasp with a lock and key. There was something about having a diary that suddenly seemed like *just* what I needed. If I had a diary, I could fill the pages with my deepest thoughts and dreams. And nobody would see what I wrote — especially nobody in my nice but nosy family.

Of course I love my family. I really think I'm lucky to have four brothers and sisters and a great mom and dad, plus a terrific grandmother who lives right upstairs. But there are times, and more and more of them lately, when I feel swamped by them, when I need to be myself, to express myself, to be The Unique Lizzie — not just "one of the Miletti bunch." I knew right away that a diary would give me someplace to be that person.

"What're you staring at?" Nancy asked, suddenly standing behind me with her new notebook.

"Nothing," I said quickly. If I told Nancy I wanted to get a diary to have a place to confide my deepest thoughts, she would probably be insulted. We were best friends after all. Why, she'd wonder, couldn't I just tell *her* these secrets, hopes and dreams, and likes and dislikes? I wasn't even sure why I couldn't. I wasn't even sure what all the stuff was that I wanted to *put* in a diary. I just knew these thoughts were there, inside me, and that they needed a secret, very private place to go.

* * *

School, in spite of it being the first day and all, looks like it's going to be a lot like last year. For history, I have Mr. Burrows again. He likes me, which is good. I need all the help I can get in history. It's my worst subject. I can never remember the date of anything — wars, treaties, the Diet of Worms, which has to be one of the grossest-sounding historical events ever. And now this year we've got more American History — a whole *new* set of dates I'm not going to be able to remember!

After history it was lunchtime, and I went down to the cafeteria to meet Nancy, who was saving a place for me. We had to protect our food through the dumbest spitball fight. Fifth-grade boys. (The worst.) And then Samantha Howard and her snooty crowd walked right past us and ignored us completely. As usual.

This year the cool crowd can't wait to get out of here and into junior high. They already dress *very* j.h. Actually, I'd like to look more junior high myself.

I'd like Samantha and her friends to look up one day as I came into the lunchroom and say, "Wow! Is that Lizzie Miletti — the girl who used to wear those dumb barrettes? She looks so *fabulous* now."

The problem is, I don't quite know how to

change myself from me into this fabulous version of me. And I don't know who to ask about it. The cool girls don't ever talk to me, so forget that. And Nancy is even less cool than I am. She wears checked tennis shoes and basically looks like she's getting dressing instructions by radio signal from another planet. She doesn't care about clothes. She thinks Samantha and her crowd are jerks and just ignores them. She never reads any of the fashion magazines. Basically, I think she doesn't want to grow up. I told her this once, and she admitted it was true.

"I love being a kid," she told me. "I'm so good at it."

I don't argue with her about this. She's right — for her. But for me it's different. I *do* want to grow up . . . a little. And even though I suppose Samantha isn't the nicest person in the world, she does dress and act the way I'd like to. Nancy just wouldn't understand this. She'd just make fun of me. So I don't talk about it. It's one of my biggest secrets, actually. I act like I couldn't care less about being cool, but really I'm dying inside, wishing I could be.

All through the day I kept finding myself thinking about you, Diary. About how you would be the private place in my life. By the time the final class bell rang, I had made up my mind to buy

11

you. I told Nancy I had to get to a piano lesson.

"I thought you only had those on Saturday."

"Usually, but this week my teacher's going to be out of town for the weekend, so I'm supposed to come today." A total lie, and it made me feel guilty. I don't usually lie to friends. But it did make Nancy back off.

I breathed a sigh of relief when Nancy finally got onto her bike and rode away. Then I was free to go to MacDermott's and buy the diary without *anyone* knowing about it.

I rushed over, handed Mr. MacDermott all of my week's lunch money, and said, "I'd like the diary. The one in the window, please."

He smiled as he went over to the window to pull it out. Old Mr. MacDermott is really nice. My mom says he sold stationery to kids at Claremont school years ago when she went there! That must have been ages ago.

"This diary is very old," he told me. "I found it a few weeks ago on a high shelf in the back of my storeroom. It must've been sitting there for thirty years. You won't see many diaries as nice as this these days. And you can see, its pages aren't dated, so you can start it anytime, and take as much space as you need for the really important days. I've been wondering if anyone would see this old beauty and appreciate its specialness."

"Do I have enough money for it?" I asked him,

spreading my bills and change out on the counter.

He looked down, nodded at me, and said, "Well, since you look to me like exactly the right girl for this particular diary, I think what you have here is exactly enough."

I thought that said something. That it was meant to be that I got a diary today. Look at how many pages I've already filled up, and this is only my first entry. I wonder how many pages of things I'll have to write about next time. It's kind of neat. Now it's like my life is this story, just waiting to be written. By me.

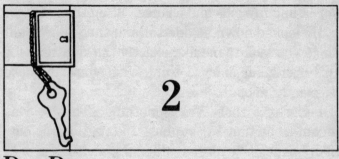

2

Dear **D**iary:

Saturday mornings, everyone at our house has to clean their rooms. Even Mom and Dad. Even Baby Rose, who just puts her toys back in their box. But still it's something. This is an absolute house rule.

"Otherwise we'll go to ruin," my mom says. "The Board of Health will arrest me and haul you all off to clean, organized foster homes."

So, although everyone moans and groans about it, we all stay in on Saturday mornings, mopping floors, and changing our beds, and sweeping under them to get out all the forgotten orange peels and cookie halves.

Today, though, while I was cleaning my room, polishing the top of my old dresser, changing the sheets, I sat down on my bed with a thump and looked around. I was hoping to feel a sense of accomplishment, but all I could feel was depressed. There simply was no ignoring it. My room is a dump.

14

It's not really even a room. When our big old frame house was built around the turn of the century, this space, under the stairs to the attic, was a dressing room off the biggest bedroom. Now, with a window stuck in one end, a door in the other, it's my room. The best thing about it is that it belongs one hundred percent to me. Adam and Josh have to share; so do Darcy and Rose. Being a middle kid has *some* advantages. But beyond privacy, there isn't much good you can say about the room. It looks pretty much like a prison cell, only without the bars.

The floor is brown linoleum, the curtains and bedspread tan corduroy. Most of the decor comes from the clown wallpaper on the end wall. My mom picked this out for me when I was five, and it's just never gotten replaced. Then there are a million horse posters and pictures I plastered all over the other walls a couple of years ago when I was deep into my horse phase. Now I never even think about horses, except when I look at my walls. Still, I don't know what to replace all this old stuff with. About the only nice thing in the room is my windowsill full of snowball paperweights. My collection. But even these look tacky in such dismal surroundings.

I know I really should do something to liven the place up, make it look sharp. But what?

When Adam poked his head in, I asked him,

"Do you think my room is okay?"

He looked around, then shrugged, "I guess so. It doesn't smell."

When Rose came toddling by, dragging my stuffed rabbit Murphy, I asked the same question.

"Oh, yes," Rose said, looking all around, then pointing toward where the wall slanted under the stairs. "It has a bended ceiling."

I sighed as I looked around again. I decided I *had* to do something about this problem. Right after my piano lesson I headed over to Singer's Drugs, where they have the biggest selection of magazines, including decorating magazines, in town.

The whole way there I practiced my walk, which I want to change. It's funny. I never even thought about my walk until one weekend when Nancy's dad took this video of us in the park, just fooling around. When we all looked at the video later, I could have died. I walk like a little kid. Like I'm on my way to the sandbox. Like I was wearing those big floppy rubber boots. It hurt to watch. Since then, every chance I get I practice my walk. I pretend I'm a fashion model walking around at a fashion show. I try to catch my reflection in store windows. Sometimes I think I'm doing all right, but once when I was out at the mall with Nancy, I was secretly practicing, and she turned and looked at me and said, "Have you got a crick in your back today?"

So I guess I still don't have it right.

Anyway, I practiced my way over to Singer's and went in. In order to look at the magazines for free, you have to first look like you're about to buy something. Otherwise Mr. Singer shoos you out of his store, telling you it's not a library. So I went to the makeup aisle to pretend to be looking for a lipstick, even though I don't wear any makeup yet. My mom would kill me.

When I came around the corner into the aisle, I saw that Samantha was there with her best friend, Candace Quinn. They were trying different blushes on the backs of their hands. Samantha and Candace *do* wear makeup. They're the best looking girls in the sixth grade, although they are different types. Samantha has long, curly blonde hair and blue eyes. Candace, on the other hand, has short black hair, a pale complexion, and green, green eyes. *So* green that people usually think she's wearing colored contacts, although she isn't.

(My eyes are green too, with long lashes. I think they're one of my beauty strong points. Well, my mom says I have nice hands, too, but somehow this doesn't seem enough to count as a beauty strong point. I mean, you never hear anyone say, "Justine Bateman is really terrific-looking. She has such great hands." My mom also says I'm going to "come into my own," lookswise, that mine are the kind of looks that will get better as I grow up. I'm really counting on this.

"Ooooo," Candace was saying, rubbing some blush on her wrist.

"*Très chic*," said Samantha.

Running into Samantha and her friends is always a problem. Since we've all known each other forever, it seems stupid just to come up and stand next to them, looking at the makeup, not saying a word. Then they might think *I* was stuck-up.

On the other hand, if I came up and said hi, I knew they'd probably snub me. It is one thing when this happens in the lunchroom when Nancy is usually there, and we can kind of laugh it off. It's much worse to face the situation alone, like now. But I took a deep breath, squared my shoulders, and told myself, Who knows? Maybe I'll come up and say hi and they'll say hi back.

With this tiny bit of courage, I walked up to them and said, "Hi, Samantha. Hi, Candace."

They didn't even look up.

I waited. Maybe they hadn't heard me. I tried again. "Hi, Samantha."

Samantha glanced up at me for a second, as though a fly was buzzing around her ear and she was just the tiniest bit distracted by it. Then she turned back to Candace and said, as though I weren't there, or as if I were invisible, "Oh, what about this one." She opened a compact of blush and smoothed some just below her thumb.

"Too red," Candace replied. I stepped backwards out of the aisle and ran out of the store, my ears burning pinker than any shade of blush on the rack.

I am a *jerk*, I thought, standing on the sidewalk, biting my lower lip to keep the tears from coming. I felt crushed, and on top of it, stupid for even trying to be nice to them.

Then, to make matters worse, my brother Adam, who is always acting like I'm just a stupid kid sister, came peeling up on his ten-speed and screeched to a halt about one inch from my foot. He always does this, just to rattle me. I was embarrassed to let him see me with dumb tears streaming down my face. I couldn't very well tell him what they were about. He thought everything girls did was too stupid for words, and if I tried to explain how hurt I was by Samantha and Candace giving me the frosty treatment, he'd just have some worthless guy-solution, like I should beat them up, or let the air out of their bike tires.

So when he said, "What's wrong?" I just said, "Nothing."

"Right," he said, not believing me for a minute.

"Well, I'm supposed to tell you Mom needs you to look after the baby for an hour or so while she gets her hair cut."

I nodded and said I'd go straight home. Then I realized I hadn't even gotten my decorating magazines. I couldn't very well go back into the store and let Samantha and Candace see me crying. I saw through the drugstore window that they were coming out toward me, so I waved good-bye to Adam and, as he raced toward the football field, I headed toward home.

On the way, I started thinking about Samantha. It's weird, really. She and Nancy and I have lived in the same neighborhood all our lives. When we were little, the three of us used to play together. But gradually Samantha pulled away from us and started hanging around with Candace and a boy-crazy crowd.

Samantha is a year older than Nancy and I are. Her birthday is on the grade dividing line. She had to either start school a little early or a little late, and her parents picked a little late. So she was seven in first grade and is twelve now. While this never seemed to bother her when we were little, now she acts like the year between her twelve and our eleven is a *huge* gap. Like she's practically grown-up and we're still babies. Nancy calls this Samantha's "superiority complex."

As I may have mentioned, Nancy just hates

Samantha and her crowd and says they are pukey morons. For a long time I felt exactly this way, too. But lately, in spite of not really liking them, I've begun to sort of want them to notice me and like me. Ask *my* opinion on blushers.

Suddenly I heard someone clearing her throat right behind me. I turned and it was her! Samantha.

"Uh . . ." I said. Sometimes I am *such* a brilliant conversationalist!

"Hi, Liz," Samantha said in the coolest voice, like liquid ice. I thought how I'd love to sound just like that. "Heading over to our neighborhood?"

"Uh, yeah," I said, keeping up my reputation as a brilliant conversationalist. To be honest, though, I was sort of in a state of shock. I mean, I don't think Samantha really has spoken to me in a year.

"Mind if I walk with you?"

"No," I said. "It's a free sidewalk."

It was a dumb, old joke, but Samantha laughed like I was Robin Williams.

"So," she said when we were walking along, "how's it going for you this year?"

I was surprised she cared, but she looked really interested. So I told her not too bad, that I was a little worried about history.

"Oh," she said, putting her hand on my arm.

"Don't worry. I'm sure you'll do fine. You've always been very smart. Remember when you spelled 'medieval' right in the fourth-grade spelling bee?"

Well, Diary, I neary fainted. Of course *I* rebembered spelling "medieval" correctly. It was one of the high points of my life. But I didn't think anyone else remembered. Especially not Samantha Howard, who I thought had forgotten my existence on the planet, not to mention my winning the fourth-grade spelling bee.

"Yeah, I'm a pretty good speller," was all I could think of to say.

"The best," Samantha said, like I'd *just* won the spelling bee, like I'd just come down off the gym stage, instead of two years ago.

By then we were at her house, which came before mine. She stopped and said good-bye.

"It was fun talking with you, Liz," she said. She had also never called me Liz before today. No one had.

I said it had been fun for me, too, or something stupid like that.

"We'll have to see each other again soon," she said. "Maybe we could eat lunch together in the cafeteria one day next week."

I just nodded, since I was speechless at this offer. I waved as she walked away (Samantha has a very smooth way of walking, of course) and then, when she got up on her front steps, before she went inside, she turned and gave me a little wave.

Even as I write this all down, Diary, it seems like something that couldn't really have happened.

Samantha Howard, being nice to me? Asking me to have lunch with her? Telling me how smart I am? Does she feel guilty because she's been so mean? Am I suddenly getting cooler and she can see it? Did she notice something different and sophisticated in my new walk? I think it has to be something like that. And I think it means I'm on my way — maybe even into the cool crowd!

I always *knew* there was something good in Samantha Howard.

3

Dear Diary:

Thursday. Rained *all* day.

Today we had a quiz in history. Mr. Burrows talked about the Boston Tea Party, and I asked if people just came out to the harbor and dipped their cups in and had iced tea. He said that since it was salt water, the tea probably would've tasted pretty terrible. Everyone laughed and I felt really good at having made a humorous remark like that.

Wore: new black pants and oversized white sweater — *no barrettes*. I'm just letting my hair go wild like it wants to, and I think it looks pretty good. The new me!

Nancy and I hung out over at her house after school. We were supposed to be doing homework, but really we were mostly playing tapes, and drying our socks on the radiator, and comparing our toes. Hers are incredibly long. I never noticed before. She can pick up a dime off the floor with them. Mine are less talented, but more regular sized.

24

"I had the weirdest experience with Samantha Saturday," I told her. I hadn't said anything about it before, because I know how Nancy feels about Samantha. But since I'd been thinking about Samantha a lot, I had to say something.

"All experiences with Samantha are weird," Nancy said. "Because Samantha is weird."

"But this wasn't like the usual Samantha experience," I tried to explain. "Well, the first part was. She and Candace snubbed me in Singer's Drugs. But then she caught up with me on the way home and was *so* chatty. You'd think we were best friends."

I could see Nancy clench up a little when I said this part about best friends. Her jaw does this little twitchy thing when she doesn't like something, but can't come out and *say* she doesn't like it. It was twitching like crazy at the moment.

Then she looked off into space and said, "I wonder what she's up to?"

"What do you mean — *up to*? Why does she have to be up to *anything*?"

"Samantha's *always* up to something."

"Maybe what she's up to is just making friends with me."

Nancy was silent for a minute and then said, "She could've been friends with you for all the time she's been snubbing you. Why suddenly does she want to be your friend?"

I didn't know what to say. The answer was so obvious — Samantha saw that I was growing and developing. Maturing. Becoming more sophisticated. I was becoming the sort of person she and her crowd would notice. I couldn't talk to Nancy about this, though. Since she thinks Samantha and her crowd are jerks and morons, she'd never understand why I want them to like me. She'd think *I* was a jerk and a moron for caring.

But I *do* care. I want to be cool. I don't want to be a nerd. Not that I really am. I'd say Nancy and I are about in the middle. We're definitely not in the Supernerd category like Tanya Malone, who brings a refrigerator carton of cold beets for lunch every day. Or Diane Eastman, who wears a trenchcoat over her shorts all through gym. Or Polly Hart, the class know-it-all.

Actually, if you define cool as good jokes and saying smart stuff, I think Nancy and I are probably cooler than Samantha. But Samantha and her friends have the cool *look*. Plus they act like they're cool, which just seems to convince everyone that they are. I don't know when this whole cool thing even started. Some time in fifth grade. And now it's like it's written in stone. Nobody gets to change places. This is one of the worst things about school. There's a new girl this year — Ericka Powell. Her family just moved here from Alaska. She hasn't made one friend. It's not that she's not nice or anything. It's just that everyone already has their friends, and they don't need to add her to the list. I'll admit I haven't really talked to her either. Once I was going to go up and just sort of casually ask her if she knew any Eskimos and if she'd ever been in an igloo. But then I didn't. I chickened out.

I'm not sure why being cool is suddenly so important to me. I guess part of it is that I think if I were, I'd get noticed more. All my life I've been like the person in the back row of a group photo. Worse, like the person in the back row who moved just as the picture was being taken, and got blurred a little. In my class I'm about in the middle, gradewise and popularitywise. At home I'm the middle kid. I'm not beautiful, not ugly. I'm not brilliant, except in spelling, which doesn't seem to count so much anymore, but I'm not dumb either. I don't usually stand out in a crowd.

But inside I *feel* unique. Special. I guess I just wish other people would notice my specialness. If I were cool and popular they would.

I can't talk to Nancy about this. She wouldn't understand. She just thinks Samantha and girls like her are superficial, and that caring about clothes and parties like they do is beneath her. And that it should be beneath me, too. She says she has *real* problems to think about. One in particular.

Now that Nancy's parents are divorced, her Dad is living down in Detroit, and she only sees him every other weekend when she goes to stay at his new apartment.

"I'd just like to go there and hack around with him," she told me today. "But he acts like he's got to entertain me all the time. Like I was Princess Di coming to America. And the mega-weird part of this is that when he lived at home, he hardly ever did anything with me. Just came home, re-moted the TV on and turned into a couch potato. Now he's Mr. Party. It's gotten so I hate to visit him. It makes me nervous, always having to show him I'm having a terrific time."

"Gee, Nancy," I said. "I've got to tell you this doesn't seem like such a giant problem to me. I mean, basically, my parents take us to the cottage on Harsen's Island for a week every summer. We swim in freezing water and eat the fish we all catch. During the year maybe we go someplace like the circus, once. And then if Mom gets ab-solutely exhausted some night, we all go out to a pizza place for dinner. That's *it* for social life around the Miletti Mansion. If *my* dad wanted to take me out to fancy French restaurants, and plays, and shopping all the time, it wouldn't be that big a problem to me. I could handle it."

Nancy got furious.

"You're not hearing what I'm saying! And

you're not being sympathetic to how upset I am. You're just seeing things from your own point of view. You're just *not* a caring friend, Lizzie Miletti!"

"But I am!" I shouted. "I'm an extremely caring friend."

"Prove it," she dared me.

"How?" I asked.

"Come with me the next time I go to visit my dad — the weekend after next. See how crazy the situation is, and try to figure out something I can do about it."

"Of course I'll go," I told her. "*Because* I'm such a caring person. And because you're my best friend. So I'd do anything for you. Even withstand the torture of a weekend of being stuffed with good food and dragged to plays and movies and stuff. I can deal with it."

In spite of the fact that she was still kind of mad at me, she laughed, and then gave me a noogie. This is her biggest sign of affection. At some point before she grows up, she's going to have to come up with something else.

Nancy, as I've said, is not maturing as fast as I am. She's like Peter Pan, refusing to grow up. For instance, she still drinks almost everything with a flexi-straw. And she has not put away her Barbie and Ken dolls. She skateboards. She makes this huge honking sound to embarrass me whenever I put a Kleenex up to my nose. Worse, when we're swimming, she pops up and squirts water at me through the space between her front teeth.

When I tell her that stuff like this just isn't cool, she says I'm getting too big for my britches. I think she's too small for hers. You'd think, being tall like she is, that her mind would go along with her body — that she'd be *more* mature than me.

Which is why Samantha is talking to me and not to Nancy. I think this makes Nancy nervous, although she'd never say so. I think she's nervous I'll get accepted into the cool crowd and desert her. I think that was the *real* argument between us. There's so much we can't say to each other lately. I wonder if this is the end of our long, long friendship?

I can't even think of that possibility. When I even get near thinking about that, I start to cry.

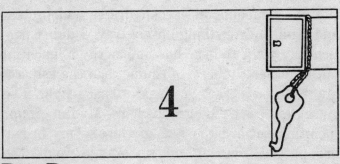

4

Dear **D**iary:

Tuesday.

Nancy was out of school today. She had to have something done at the orthodontist, and he was miles away. Braces are a bore! She was happy to have a day off, but for me it was a drag. No one to go to school with, no one to come home with. No one to sit with at lunch.

Plus, I'd been too rushed to pack a sandwich this morning, so I was just hoping the hot lunch wouldn't be too gross.

No luck. Today they were serving the worst menu of them all — what everybody calls the Lunch From Hell. Fish croquettes with creamed onions. Tapioca pudding for dessert.

So I pushed my tray past the steaming pans and just took a bag of chips, a brownie, and a carton of orange drink.

"A well-balanced meal, I see," said Robert Wilkins, who was behind me in line.

Robert is a science brain, and probably knew

the exact amount of carbohydrates and protein and stuff in everything on my tray. I didn't particularly want to hear how unhealthy a lunch I'd put together. Robert, of course, had the fish croquettes on *his* tray. So I said, "That's right. I've got all my basic food groups here. My tan group" (pointing toward the bag of chips), "my brown group" (the brownie), "and my orange group" (the orange drink).

"Ha ha ha," Robert said sarcastically, but I knew I'd gotten him, and walked off before he could think of anything clever to say back to me.

I found an empty table off in the corner and set my tray down. I'd brought a decorating magazine, *Bedroom Projects*, along with me. I was hoping maybe it would give me some ideas for my prison cell. Most of the articles involved putting in platform beds or lofts or bookshelves — stuff that would take a degree in carpentry and about a thousand dollars, but finally I found one girl's room that had been completely made over (there were "before" and "after" pictures) into a warm, peach-colored place with a blue-and-white patchwork quilt and bright prints of paintings on the wall. It was really perfect.

I must have been staring at the pictures pretty

carefully because I didn't hear or see anyone come up to the table.

"So how's it going, Liz? I just saw you over here all by yourself and thought you might want a little company," Samantha said sweetly. "But I see you're busy reading . . ."

"Oh, no. Please. Sit down."

"You planning some decorating?" Samantha asked, picking up the magazine and looking at the pictures.

"My bedroom's like a prison cell," I said.

Samantha nodded, opening a can of pop, then picking up a fry and munching it. All she'd taken for lunch was fries with ketchup.

"I just decorated mine last year. Maybe I could help you. Give you some tips."

"Wow! That'd be great," I said. I was amazed that I didn't feel too uptight with Samantha, after all this time of hating her and kind of fearing her from afar at the same time. The problem obviously was Nancy. Samantha felt uncomfortable with Nancy and so she didn't talk to me. I mean, look at the evidence. Today, as soon as I was sitting in the lunchroom by myself, Samantha had come over to talk.

"Is this the room you want?" Samantha said, pointing to the photo in the magazine.

I nodded.

"It's a little *young*, isn't it?"

I felt myself blushing and looked back down at the photo. Actually, I'd been thinking it was the absolutely *perfect* room, but now, trying to look at the picture through Samantha's sophisticated eyes, I could see that maybe it *was* a little childish. Maybe. Sort of.

"I was going to ask my gram to come pick out the stuff with me," I started to tell Samantha. "She lives with us and has her own apartment in the attic decorated really nice. All soft colors . . ."

"You're going to let your *grandmother* help you decorate your room!?" Samantha squealed. "Give me a break. What do you want — doilies on everything? An old rocking chair?"

"Uh, well, Gram's not that kind of grandmother." I felt a little strange. I really love Gram, and she is definitely not your average grandmother. She's a very special person, and especially special to me. *And* she has great taste. But I didn't feel I could explain all this to Samantha, so I just let it slide. But I felt I *should* be defending Gram.

"I know!" Samantha said. "You could try to get your grandmother to come up with the money for all the things you'll need. Money is usually something grandparents are good for. If you get enough out of her for drapes and a new spread

34

and some decorations, I'd go to the mall with you on Saturday and help you pick the stuff out."

I was really torn. I didn't like the idea of "getting money out of" Gram. I'd never done anything like that before. Usually if she gives me anything, it's a gift — something *she's* thought up, not me. I like it better that way. On the other hand, if I could get some decorating money from her, I could spend a whole afternoon shopping with Samantha. That was the kind of thing really good friends did together. The kind of things the girls in the cool crowd do together.

Maybe Samantha and I would meet Candace and their friend Jessica afterward. Have a Coke at the McDonald's at the mall. Maybe this was their casual way of letting me into the in crowd. And maybe if I didn't get the money from Gram and go along with Samantha on Saturday, I'd miss my one big chance to get in.

"I'll try," I told Samantha in the end.

"Well, call me when you know," she said. "The sooner the better. My social schedule gets kind of full on the weekends. But if you get the money, I'd love to help you pick out some things."

I looked up at the huge wall clock. It was already time to go. I am pretty sure the clock in the lunchroom runs fast, and the clocks in the classrooms run slow, but I can't prove this. I smiled my way across the lunchroom as I waved good-bye to Samantha and went to return my tray.

I walked straight to Nancy's house after school. I couldn't wait to tell her all about my lunch with Samantha. I guess I wanted to prove she was wrong for being suspicious. Clearly Samantha just liked me — for myself.

No one was home, though, so I sat down on the front porch steps to wait. It was almost an hour before Nancy's mother's station wagon came around the corner and pulled into the drive. The car was barely parked when Nancy sprung out like a jack-in-the-box.

She ran up to me, grinned, and said, "Well?"

I thought maybe she'd heard about me and Samantha having lunch together and wanted to know all about it. So I rushed right into the whole story. When I was done, I waited for Nancy's reaction.

I didn't know what to expect, but was I ever shocked when Nancy spit out at me, "Lizzie Miletti! You are *so* self-absorbed! You're all huffed and puffed up with this stupid story about *Samantha*. You haven't even noticed."

"Noticed what?" I said.

Nancy narrowed her eyes until they were just an angry squint.

"My perm."

It was undeniably true. Nancy's hair had definitely gone from absolutely straight to nearly as curly as mine. And it was also undeniably true that I hadn't noticed.

"I . . . uh . . ."

"Samantha," Nancy said the name through her nose, making it sound awful. "I've just made a major change in my image, and all you can talk about is Samantha Howard. You'll pardon me if I don't want to stay out here and listen to any more of this *fascinating* story. I'm going inside to comb my perm. It was my mom's idea. I'm still not sure about it. I got done at the orthodontist early, so Mom took me to the beauty parlor."

"Hey," I said, grabbing Nancy by the arm. "It looks great. Really. Terrific. I must have just been so stunned by how great it looks that I blocked it out or something." The truth was I thought it looked horrible. Almost as horrible as my own frizzy hair. But I wanted to be encouraging. Nancy getting *anything* changed about her appearance was definitely something unusual. Maybe there was hope. Maybe she was getting into style, even if it was a hideous style.

"You really think its's okay?" Nancy said, pushing at it with her hand.

"Really. A lot like Sigourney Weaver's hair."

"Really?" Nancy said.

"Yeah, kind of rumpled, like at the end of *Aliens* after she's killed all the drooly monsters."

Nancy's response to this was — giving me a noogie. So much for my thought that maybe she was growing up. Today, though, I didn't really care. I was just happy she wasn't mad at me anymore. I hate it when that happens.

"Did you ask your parents about coming to my dad's with me?" she asked then.

"Oh, boy. I forgot." I slapped my forehead, feeling like a double-rotten friend. Then I promised, "I will tonight. They'll say yes. They like your dad and they think it's good that I go different places. Expanding my horizons, they call it."

I didn't mention anything more about Samantha. It's clearly a touchy subject. Off-limits.

Dear **D**iary:

It's late. Everyone else is asleep.

Well, I did it. Last night I went up to talk to Gram about redecorating my room. I really hated asking her for the money, but it was the only way I could go shopping with Samantha.

I just love going up to Gram's apartment in the attic. It's so pretty, and it's also the only quiet place in the house.

Tonight when I went up, Gram was in her little living room, watching TV and knitting this sock that looked like it was for Big Foot. She's teaching herself to knit. So far she's just made this lumpy scarf for Dad, and now this sock. I don't think she's going to turn out to be a great knitter, but I never mention this. I am a very tactful person.

I sat down on the sofa across from her and she flipped the TV off with the remote control. She always gives me her total attention when I have something I need to talk about. And I can talk to her about almost anything. She would never tell anyone — not even if it's about being mad at my mother, who is her own daughter.

In a lot of ways, Gram is the person I'm closest to in the family. We even share the same name — Elizabeth — only, people call me Lizzie, and they call her Betty. We go places together all the time. She sells real estate, and sometimes she takes me along when she's showing a house to some possible buyers. On weekends we drive out to antique shops, where I look for snowball paperweights, and we both look at the old postcards. Some of them have writing on the back — messages from vacations taken a million years ago. It's kind of weird reading these, like I'm spying on someone else's life.

Other times we go swimming together at the Y. Gram used to be on the synchronized swim team at her high school, and she can still do underwater somersaults.

Sometimes on weeknights after dinner, we'll go to the library. We both get stacks of books, then go next door to Edna's Coffee Pot. Gram has known Edna for about a hundred years, so we always get extra ice cream on our slices of pie (for free). We sit in the booth by the front window and talk about everything. Well, almost everything. I don't tell her when I'm mean to Darcy, or when I ignore Rose. Gram has this idea that

I'm just a terrific sister, and so when I'm not I don't let her know. I like to keep up my image.

She's really more than just a grandmother to me — more like my special friend. She likes my brothers and sisters, too, but she pays lots of extra attention to me, and it's really the one thing that makes me feel singled out around this house. Dad's on the road selling most of the time, and Mom's so busy managing the house and taking care of the baby and all . . . well, they're spread pretty thin. But Gram always has time for me, or makes time even if she doesn't really have it.

Like tonight. As soon as I told her about my room being a dump, she got really into fixing it up. She put her knitting down in her lap and closed her eyes, trying to visualize my room and help me with some ideas to make it better.

"What style do you have in mind?" she asked me. "What look? What colors?"

I told her I had in mind a cozy, country-cottage look.

"Oh, that sounds so sweet," she said, and started making a list of the things I'd need. A patchwork spread. A little lamp made out of a pitcher.

"I saw one that's just perfect at the mall," she said, then smiled with her great idea. "I know! Why don't we make an expedition? A shopping trip out to the mall. Say on Saturday?"

"Well, I, uh . . ." I stammered. "See, the thing is, I kind of planned to go with a friend . . ."

"Nancy?" Gram said. "Well, bring her along. The three of us always have so much fun together."

"Well, it's not exactly Nancy," I said. "It's Samantha."

"Samantha Howard? I thought you and Nancy hated her like poison."

"Well, Nancy still hates her, but I'm not so sure about myself. She's really being nice to me lately."

"And it's hard to hate someone who's being nice to you," Gram said.

I nodded and agreed.

"It is, isn't it?"

"Well, that's great," she said. "I've always been sorry that Samantha turned into such a snooty little thing. I'm glad to see she's coming around again."

Gram didn't seem the least bit suspicious of Samantha's wanting to be my friend. Not like Nancy was. Of course, I should say that Gram always thinks the best of everybody. I mean even when there's some big murder in the newspapers, she always says the murderer must be a sad, troubled person, and probably just hadn't gotten enough love as a child.

"Maybe Samantha's getting more mature,"

Gram said then. "She certainly *looks* grown up these days."

"Yeah," I said. "I guess that's how I'd like to look. She's one of the cool crowd at school. They all dress great and have parties and know just the right things to say. I think . . ." I stopped here. I didn't want to sound conceited. But Gram urged me on.

"You think what?"

"Well, I think they may want me in their crowd. I think that may be why Samantha's being friendly with me lately."

Gram just nodded for a while, then she asked me. "And it's important to you to get into this crowd?"

I just nodded. I didn't want to sound gushy about how excited I was. I think she could tell, though, from my expression. I'm not much of a poker face.

"Well, then," Gram said, getting up out of her chair and going over to get her purse. "I always like you to have what makes you happy. What about a little cash for your redecorating?"

I gulped when I looked down at the money Gram pressed into my hand. There were three twenty-dollar bills. More than I expected. Somehow, though, this just made me feel worse for going shopping without her.

"Just invite me down for a cup of tea in your 'country cottage' when it's all fixed up," she said. For some reason this made me want to cry. Which I did as soon as I was out of her sight. I had tears streaming down my cheeks as I walked slowly down the attic stairs back into the house. I just felt totally rotten. And in some way, I wished I *were* going to the mall with Gram.

Then, in the lunchroom today when Samantha came up to me and asked, "So, did you get your granny to cough up some money?" I felt double rotten for letting her talk about Gram and me in such a creepy way. But I just said yes, and she gave me a hug and smiled her super-friendliest smile.

"Then we're on for Saturday. We can do the mall, then go over to the Zephyr for a little ice cream. Maybe meet some of the others."

And suddenly I just pushed Gram out of my mind and let it fill up with a picture of all the girls in the cool crowd sitting around me in the Zephyr, ooohing and ahhing over all my new bedroom stuff, and at what great taste we had — me and my new friend Samantha!

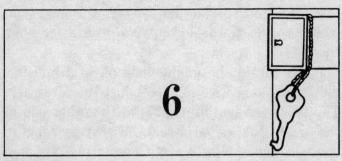

6

Dear **D**iary:

What a day I've just been through!

It started perfectly ordinary — just like any other Saturday. I cleaned my room and went for my piano lesson. But then at two, I met Samantha over at the mall to shop for my room. I had to wait half an hour for her. She didn't apologize for being so late or anything. She just said, "Hey." All the cool kids say "hey" now instead of "hi." But she could have said she was sorry for being late, too.

My plan was to go to the Country Shoppe, this nice little store where everything has a country look to it. Gingham print pillows and curtains. Patchwork spreads. Lamps shaped like little ducks. But when I started to go inside, she grabbed my arm.

"What do you want to go in that corny place for?" Samantha asked.

"But . . ."

"Come on. You want your room to look like

something out of Mother Goose? I'll show you where to get the look you *really* need for your room."

I was afraid she might walk off in a huff if I didn't go along with her, so I just ran after her. The store she had in mind is at the other end of the mall. It's called FreakOut. Everything in there is kind of New Wave. Chairs padded in gold vinyl. Neon clocks. Lots of stuff in weird colors like lime green and violent orange. Also a lot of things in fake animal prints. Samantha managed to find both a bedspread and curtains in this plushy, leopard-spotted material.

Argh, I thought, but I didn't say anything when she told me, "These are just perfect for your new room."

At first I thought she was joking, but then I could see she wasn't. I tried to think of some way to tell her I thought they were ugly, but I didn't want to insult her taste.

"Uh . . . I don't think my parents will let me get anything that wild," I said. I've found that when I can't get out of something, I can usually put the blame on my parents.

"What are you, some kind of wimp?" she said. "A baby who lets her mother and father pick how her own room is going to look?"

"Well, no, but . . ."

"No buts," she said, then shouted, "Oh, here it

is! The perfect lamp!" She rushed across the store to this lamp that had a base which was a glass tube with a giant blob of something slowly going up and down in orange liquid. I thought I was going to get seasick just looking at it.

"Oh, great!" she shouted, picking it up.

"Samantha," I said, weakly. "I think maybe I'm just too old-fashioned for this decor."

"Don't be silly," she said in this crisp voice, like she was the professional decorator and knew best. She even patted my head like I was a little kid. "Once we get this all together in your room, you'll see how right I am. You won't just have a decor, you'll be making a *style statement*."

But will I be able to sleep without nightmares? I wondered.

Don't ask me, Diary, how I let Samantha completely bulldoze me in that store. But I did. I guess it just all happened so fast. And I thought maybe Samantha was right and I was just out of style. The next thing I knew we were on our way out with our arms full of shopping bags and *without* most of Gram's money. To be exact, we had just enough left for a gallon of paint in the "perfect" (according to Samantha) color. Lime green.

We didn't even get to stop at the Zephyr for ice cream with the cool crowd.

"Can't," Samantha said. "We've got to get this

paint on the walls and put your new look together."

On the way out of the mall we passed the Coffee & Tea Room, and I looked in to see Gram having tea and cake with Nancy. They're pretty good friends, and I guess since I was busy they'd decided to just get together without me. They were deep in some conversation. I was dying to know what they were talking about. Actually, I was dying to be with them at the little marble-topped table, with my sixty dollars in my pocket, on my way to the Country Shoppe to buy my patchwork quilt and little lamp shaped like a milk pitcher.

Then Nancy looked up and saw me and Samantha rushing by with all our bags. She didn't even wave or smile. She just looked back down and stared at her ice cream. I've never felt so lonely or shut out in my life.

Samantha and I spent the rest of the afternoon painting and putting up the curtains. She planned everything — even rearranged my furniture. I felt like a total wimp, but I also thought she must know what she's doing.

Then I helped her put the spread on the bed and plug the lamp in next to it. I stood back and looked at what we had done.

"Well, it certainly is a change," I said. It was the best I could do. I was heartsick, but didn't want Samantha to see that. She had put so much time into helping me out with this. How could I tell her that my poor little room, which had only looked like a prison cell before, now looked like the Fun House I'd gone to once at an amusement park?

By now my siblings were starting to come around to see the decorating project. Josh was too cool to comment. He just raised his eyebrows as he walked past.

Adam stopped and said, "Far *out*."

"Oh," Samantha said to him, then giggled in this way I'd never heard her laugh before. "Do you really like it?"

"I didn't say that," Adam said. "I just said it was far out." He was doing his "tough guy" thing. I was afraid Samantha would be insulted, but she just stood there, hanging on his words as he walked off. Adam is, as Mom says, "moody." She says it's because his hormones are changing and that when I hit puberty my hormones will be all out of whack, too, and I'll act weird. But I doubt it. I think I'm just going to go on just like I am until I'm an old person, only somewhere along the way I'm going to "come into my looks" like Mom says I will.

I thanked Samantha for being nice to Adam.

"He's moody, I know," I said.

She didn't say anything about this, just watched him walk off down the hallway toward his room.

I could tell she thought he was too weird to comment on.

Then Darcy came up the stairs with Baby Rose. "Gross," was her one-word review of the room.

Baby Rose had an even simpler opinion. She took one long look and burst out crying.

Those were my feelings exactly. What have I done? I thought. And what have I done with Gram's money? And how have I hurt Nancy by totally leaving her out of this project and letting her see me buddy-buddy with Samantha this afternoon?

After Samantha left, assuring me I now had "the most unusual bedroom of any girl at Claremont," I just wanted to shut the door and lie face down on my stupid leopard-print bed and cry my eyes out.

But I couldn't. Mom and Dad, and then Gram, all came by to see the room. Although I was dying on the inside, I had to sit there and do this Academy Award-winning performance, pretending this was exactly how I wanted my room, that I was pleased as could be with it.

But now I'm alone, Diary. It's late at night and no one's around. So if you'll excuse me, I'm going to stop writing for now so I can just sit here and cry at having been the biggest dope in the world. About the only good thing that came of all this is that now Samantha really seems to be my friend. Pretty soon, I'm going to be part of the cool crowd. I guess that's worth paying the price of having to live in the weirdest bedroom in the world.

Maybe in the universe.

7

Dear **D**iary:

Things are getting stranger and stranger between me and Nancy. We used to think alike on almost everything. We were best friends sometimes because we liked the same things, but other times because we hated the same things. Or the same people. We hated Samantha together for years before this year when I started to like her. We used to like chocolate ice cream best, but now we like coconut. We used to like gym when it was just playing Red Rover or Duck, Duck, Goose, or jumping rope out on the playground. But starting last year, it got all organized and Nancy and I began to hate it with a passion. This year it's the same thing — aerobics. With the same teacher — Mrs. Nelson. We hate her, too.

Behind her back, we call her Jane Honda, because she's built stocky like a car and thinks she's the exercise queen. We make some pretty funny jokes about her. Like when she shouts, "All right everybody, let's burn it! Let's hit the wall!"

I usually say to Nancy, "I'd rather hit the hay!"

And then I dive onto my exercise mat. This cracks me and Nancy up, but usually gets us a big glare from Mrs. Nelson, who takes aerobics *very* seriously.

Someone else who takes aerobics seriously is Samantha. And Candace. And their friend Jessica. They think aerobics is kind of health-clubby and grown up. Plus, it gives them a chance to wear their ultra-chic aerobic workout outfits.

Nancy and I laugh at these outfits. We ourselves try to wear our worst, scuzziest, most tattered and torn old cut-offs and T-shirts. Today, though, I had made a few changes. Instead of old shorts and a T-shirt, I'd brought a black leotard I had from some ballet lessons Gram had signed me up for last year. Over this I wore a pair of red shorts and a good T-shirt from my summer vacation that says "Harsen's Island" on it with a picture of waves. I'd also borrowed a black headband from my brother Josh, who's a runner. Standing in the changing room, looking at myself in the mirror, I knew I looked pretty good. But I was afraid to come out into the gym.

I hadn't told Nancy anything about this outfit. I knew she'd be out there in a grayish T-shirt with pizza stains and her ratty corduroy cut-offs with a million threads hanging down her legs. I also knew I should have said something to her before just showing up at class in this outfit. But I'd been afraid she'd make fun of me. And now it was too late.

"Girls! Girls!" Mrs. Nelson shouted into the changing room. "Let's get out there and burn it!"

I walked slowly out into the gym. From across the room I could see Nancy's jaw dropping. When I got to her, neither of us said anything. It wasn't just my outfit. It was what it *meant*. We both knew it meant I wanted to look more like Samantha and her friends, and less like Nancy and I always have.

Neither of us said anything. Nancy just stood there, getting madder and madder and then finally she just jogged off by herself for the running part of the class. I ran after her.

When I caught up, I said, between panting (I am a terrible runner), "It doesn't really mean anything," I tried to tell her. "I just felt like a change."

"But these changes are all making you less like you — less like *us*."

"But what's so terrible about change?" I asked her.

"It's terrible if the changes are all making you more and more like the girls I hate. The girls *you* used to hate, too. And so you'll excuse me if I do the rest of my run by myself. You'll probably want to join your new friend anyway." She nodded behind us to show she meant Samantha. Then she said, "You probably want to do some more shopping with her this weekend — instead of coming to Detroit with me."

"No! I still want to come with you," I told her.

"Then you finally asked your parents?"

"Well . . ."

"You forgot again?"

"I'm sorry. I'll do it tonight. I promise."

"You don't care . . ."

"But I do . . ." I said, and then I couldn't say anything more because someone had come up and was jogging alongside us. Nancy looked over, and I saw disgust come across her face, so I knew it had to be Samantha. She was with Candace.

"Hey Liz," Samantha said. "Neat outfit."

"Yeah, Liz," Candace agreed. "Really cool."

"Liz?!" Nancy said. She'd never heard anyone call me that before.

"So, how's it going?" Samantha said then.

"Oh, fine."

"Do you just love your room? I hope you think I helped."

I hadn't shown the room to Nancy yet. I was too embarrassed. I knew she'd think it was stupid, and guess that Samantha had pushed me into doing it. So I couldn't look Nancy in the eye at the moment. Instead, I smiled at Samantha and lied.

"Oh, yeah. It looks great. You'll have to come see it sometime," I said to Candace.

"You know what you should do to celebrate it?" Samantha said in her "I'm so excited" voice.

"What?" I said.

"Have a slumber party!"

"Oh," I said. I'd never had a party of any kind, much less one where lots of girls would be staying over a whole night. It just seemed way beyond me, socially. But I didn't know exactly how to explain this to Samantha. And I didn't want to put a wet blanket on her idea, so I just said, "I'll have to see if my mom will let me."

"Be sure to let me know when you decide to have it," Samantha said, acting like it was all settled. Nancy barely waited until Samantha and Candace had jogged off ahead before she stuck out her tongue to make a barf sign.

"Give me a break," she said.

"What do you mean?" I said. "It's not such a bad idea. I don't give enough parties."

"To be exact, you don't give *any* parties," Nancy said. "And don't tell me you're going to start now just because her highness Samantha comes over here and gives the royal summons."

"She's just trying to be friendly."

"She's got some devious motive, I know it!"

"Some friend you are!" I said. "What you're really saying is that no one could just be interested in me. They'd have to be interested in me for some *other* reason." I was really mad!

"I would not say that about anyone but Samantha, who always has a devious reason for *everything* she does."

"You just hate her."

"Of course I hate her."

"And," I said, glaring at Nancy, "maybe you're also just a little bit jealous?"

"Jealous?!"

"Yes. Of Samantha Howard. My new friend. Maybe my new *best* friend."

As the words came out of my mouth, I wanted to cry. I watched Nancy run on ahead. She didn't look back.

Oh, Diary, what have I done?

I still can't stop thinking about the expression on Nancy's face as she ran off. It's like my brain is this videorecorder that keeps playing the whole terrible scene over and over again.

Why did I do it? Why would I be mean to Nancy, of all people — Nancy, who is never mean to me? Why am I selling her out just to get some attention from Samantha and her friends, who have always been just awful to me?

When I look at it in this way, I feel like a total

crumb. But then I think about how Nancy wants to stay a kid forever. Maybe Samantha is kind of a jerk, but at least she and her crowd are changing with the times. Nancy wants to play the same old games, ride her bike, do her bird-watching (her big hobby). Except for being taller (and getting that perm, and it's hard to tell if that's a step forward, or a step back), she still looks and dresses the same as she has for years. Sometimes I can even imagine her competely grown up — going to some big corporate job — dressed in purple high-tops, baggy old jeans, her T-shirt that says "My grandma got me this at Disneyland," and E.T. underwear.

She's just so exasperating. And not only is she a stick-in-the-mud, but she wants me stuck in the same mud. If I make even the tiniest little change in my appearance, or want to try something new, she acts like I'm about to become a clone of Samantha. And like it's this big betrayal of her.

When I think about it this way, I can get pretty steamed.

Still.

She *is* my best friend. She *has* stuck with me through thick and thin. *She* would never snub me. And yet today I was totally mean to her. I wouldn't be surprised if she never spoke to me again in our lives. She'd have a right just to abandon me forever. Thinking about this possibility makes me *so* sad. See these? I'll circle them for posterity.

Tears cried by Lizzie Miletti because she was so dumb that she lost her best friend.

8

Dear **D**iary:

I woke up this morning knowing I had to apologize to Nancy, but nervous about doing it. I hate it when we're not speaking to each other. It's like there's something wrong with my world, and I can't even think straight until I get it right again.

I got dressed in half my usual time and rode my bike like lightning over to her house (this was no time to try to look cool). But she was already gone. The garage was open and her bike was missing.

When I got to school I looked all over for her. But when I finally found her, she was in talking with Mr. Burrows. Probably about her extra-credit project in history. Something on the pilgrims. Nancy really works hard for her grades. Unlike me. I basically use the "flake off" and "coast through" methods. Especially in history, which — as I may have said before — I hate.

Which is probably why I'm flunking it. It's true.

I've already flunked the two quizzes we've had. I just can't seem to care *when* things happened, or what the things were. I can't *relate* to Paul Revere or Dolly Madison.

Nancy's exactly the opposite. She just loves thinking about historical times. Merry old England. Ancient Egypt. She says she loves imagining what it would have been like to be Cleopatra or Queen Elizabeth I. When she talks like this, it almost makes me interested in history. Almost. But then I get back in Burrows' class and I'm falling asleep again.

Anyway, I couldn't very well burst into the room while she was talking with Burrows this morning. And then the bell rang for classes, so I didn't have another chance to try to catch her until lunch.

Luckily (for me), she was sitting by herself when I got there. I put my tray on the table across from her and sat down. She looked at me but didn't say anything. I knew she wouldn't. I knew I could sit there for five years, and, unless I came up with an apology, she wouldn't speak to me. Nancy is very tough when she's really mad. And she was *really* mad today.

I told her I was really sorry. She still didn't say anything.

"Can you forgive me?"

"I *could*," she said. "But what proof would I

61

have that you wouldn't do it again?"

"I just wouldn't," I told her.

"Promise," she said.

I stretched my hand over to Nancy to promise.

"I promise I will never ever again say that Samantha Howard is my best friend because she never could be. That position is — and always will be — occupied by Nancy B. Underpeace."

"What does the B stand for?" Nancy asked.

"Bestfriend," I said.

She couldn't resist smiling. And then we started giggling. We are each other's best audience. Our jokes crack us up even when other people are standing around going, "hunh?"

I knew then that things were going to be all right — at least for the time being.

After we stopped laughing, we were just quiet together for a little while, then Nancy said, "Did you ask your mom about coming with me this weekend?"

I figured she was going to ask me this, so I was prepared.

"Yeah. And she says it's all right. I'll start planning my travel wardrobe tonight — that is, if you still want me to come."

"I still want you. Even though you're a rotten best friend sometimes, you're still the only best friend I've got. Plus, you know my dad and maybe you can help me figure out what's going on with him. I can't think straight about it anymore. And I don't have any idea how to get things back to normal. That's what I'm counting on you for."

I just nodded with a lot of confidence, like I was chock-full of terrific ideas. Inside I was thinking:
??????
Because I didn't have one single idea of how to solve Nancy's problem. I'm just hoping something will come to me when we're in Detroit.

Boy, Diary, do I have a lot on my mind these days.

1. Helping Nancy.

2. Staying friends with Samantha even though she seems to be ruining my life.

3. Passing history.

4. Asking Mom about having the slumber party.

5. Getting my room back to normal.

Well, I guess I'll use the method I usually do when I have too many worries pressing on my mind. Go to sleep.

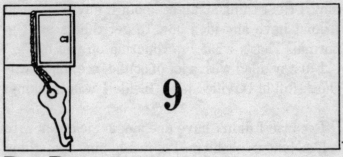

9

Dear **D**iary:

Just back from Detroit, and am I tired! I'm not sure I'll be able to tell you all about the weekend with Nancy and her dad — much less make sense of it. But I'll try.

Friday morning I packed a little suitcase with all of what I felt were my three *best* outfits, and on Friday afternoon Nancy's mother drove us to downtown Detroit. Nancy's father's an architect and has an office high up in a building that looks down on the river. Along the walls are shelves with models of all the buildings he's designed. Her dad is kind of an artistic-looking type but a great dresser. He has blond hair like Nancy, and glasses with skinny frames.

We had to wait until he finished an important phone call, and then we waited some more while he had a little talk with Nancy's mom. I thought they acted very friendly with each other — not like two people who are supposed to not get along and be divorced.

When Nancy's mom finally left, Nancy's dad turned and looked at us and said, "Are we having fun yet?"

I thought this was pretty funny, but I saw Nancy wince. He gave her a quick hug and then suggested the three of us go for dinner at a Chinese restaurant.

The restaurant turned out to be across the river, in Windsor, Ontario. That's in Canada. We had to go through customs and say we were born in the United States when the guard asked us. I thought it was kind of neat. And then we went over the bridge and had dinner in a foreign country (sort of).

It was a great Chinese restaurant. There is one in Hampton Point, where we live, but it's pretty American. You can get chow mein or chop suey or burgers. The restaurant in Windsor has a waterfall inside, and Nancy's dad got us fruit punch that came in real pineapples. I didn't recognize one thing on the menu and neither did Nancy, so her dad just did all the ordering.

Everything was good — weird, but good. I didn't want to be an insensitive friend, but really, at that point I couldn't see what Nancy's problem was. *I* was having a great time. I opened everybody's fortune cookies and then made up their fortunes. For myself, I made up: YOU ARE GOING TO FLUNK HISTORY.

Nancy was quiet through dinner, but I didn't have a chance to talk with her alone so I couldn't be sure what she was thinking.

Her dad had tickets for all of us to go to a play. I had only been to two other plays in my life. One was the *Wizard of Oz* at the Hampton Point Children's Theater. The other was when Mom took me to see *Cats* two birthdays ago. Both were musicals. This play Nancy's dad took us to see was kind of the opposite of a musical.

There were only three people in it. One of them was sitting in a garbage can. Another was in a sandbox. And the third one was dressed in black. He was supposed to be Death. I didn't understand much of what the play was about.

"You can tell it has tons of Deeper Message, but this message is going right by me," I told Nancy at intermission when her dad was away for a minute.

"The message of this whole *night* is going right by you," she said.

"What do you mean?" I asked her.

"Can't you see how my dad is so busy playing camp counsellor that he never asks me anything about how I'm doing, what I'm thinking, what I feel?"

I stopped to think about this. "I guess you're right," I told her. Then Mr. Underpeace was back, and I didn't have any more chances to talk with her.

When the play was over, her dad drove us back to his apartment. He asked what everyone thought of the play.

Nancy didn't say anything. I wanted him to know I appreciated him taking us and all, so I tried to sound intelligent. I said I enjoyed the deeper message, and hoped that was a good comment. I wanted to sound like I understood drama.

And then everybody in my dreams that night was sitting in a garbage can, so I figured maybe the deeper message *did* reach me.

Nancy and I slept in the room her dad kept for her in his apartment. I expected we'd all sleep in on Saturday. Nancy and I are champs at sleeping in. But it was pretty bright and early when her dad came in and shouted, "Hey! Are we having fun yet?"

We both rolled over and groaned.

Mr. Underpeace had about a jillion plans for the day. First we went to a delicatessen and had hot bagels (my new favorite food!), then to the Institute of Arts, where we saw what seemed to me about two thousand paintings and statues. I love art, though, and felt very artistic just walking around in there. I asked Nancy what she thought of this painting and that, but she only shrugged as though she couldn't care less.

Then we went to a super-modern shopping mall, and I got a ceramic pin that said *Liz*, and I insisted Nancy have her picture taken with her favorite star, Tom Cruise. It was really only a cardboard cutout, but it looked incredibly real.

When the picture was developed I looked at it, then looked closer, and I saw Nancy was crying. I looked over at her, and she still was!

"Oh, Nancy," I said. "What's the matter?" Her dad was there when this happened, but he didn't say anything. He just pretended he hadn't noticed. I think he was embarrassed. I gave Nancy a Kleenex and a hug as we walked to the parking lot and got into her dad's car.

I thought we were going back to the apartment, but her father still wanted us to see the zoo. He took pictures of us with all the animals, and told jokes the whole time, trying to cheer Nancy up, I guess. And of course he asked if we were having fun yet.

When Nancy went into the ladies' room, Mr. Underpeace and I were alone for a while out by the lion cages. He turned to me and said, "What's wrong with Nancy? Is it something I said?"

I didn't know how to tell him it was all the things he *didn't* say. I didn't want to be rude. "Gee, Mr. Underpeace."

"Call me Ted."

I couldn't. I am only eleven. I just can't call adults by their first names. A couple of them have asked me, but I just can't do it. It sounds fake to my ears. I also couldn't talk to Nancy's dad about Nancy's problem. I wanted to. And I knew if I did, maybe things would begin to straighten out for them. But I just couldn't think of the right words.

This was like some high-level diplomatic situation, and I was afraid I'd blurt everything out the wrong way and hurt his feelings. So I just lied and said Nancy was nervous about her schoolwork. Sometimes I am *such* a wimp. Some best friend I am, but like I said, I'm only eleven.

That night we went to see a French movie at a college film society. It had the English translation of what everyone was saying, at the bottom of the screen. Nancy's father was the kind of person who knew all about these out-of-the-way sort of entertainment events. As opposed to *my* parents, who pretty much stick to whatever is out on video this month.

After the movie, Nancy's dad wanted to have a lively discussion about it. I tried to duck his questions since I had not been able to tell whether the two main characters were brother and sister, or two people who had just met on a train. I was way too embarrassed to admit this. Plus, I was way too tired to talk about anything. All I could think of was bed, the way people crawling across deserts can only think of water. And so it was a pretty weird conversation with me too tired to talk and Nancy still not speaking except in yeses and nos when her dad really pressed her.

When we were in her room, Nancy said, "See?"

"Yeah," I admitted. "I do now. I think partly you're just tired out by these weekends, plus there's no real time for you to just *be* with your dad. Just hanging out, the way kids are supposed to be with their parents — where you don't have to pay attention to each other every single minute."

"Right," she said. "But what can I do? I don't think he even *notices* how miserable I am."

I didn't want to say that he did, because then I'd have to tell Nancy about my conversation with him. Or rather my *non*-conversation, since I had completely missed my chance to talk to him and help her out. I didn't want her to know I'd failed her. This whole situation was getting way too complicated. I was starting to get a headache from being caught in the middle.

Plus, the other thing I couldn't really tell her is that I have mixed feelings about her problem. I mean, now that I've been through a weekend of "Life in the Fast Lane with Dad," I can see why

70

Nancy feels distant from her father, and lonely — even when she's with him.

On the other hand, being with Nancy's dad is sure a lot more fun than being with *my* dad, who is usually either on the road, or home and tired out, or focused on some weird new frozen food, or trying to deal with *all* us kids, and no time to give individual attention to any *one* of us.

The last time I got to do something with just him was in fourth grade when I broke my arm in the playground and he came to the principal's office to pick me up and take me to the hospital to have the bone set. Not one of the *most* treasured memories in my scrapbook, if you know what I mean.

I guess the perfect father would be somewhere between Nancy's dad and mine. I know I have to find a way to help Nancy get her dad to pay her some *real* attention, instead of just being kind of like a human Disneyland around her. I'm not sure what that way is, though. I think I'll ask Gram. She's great on personal problems.

Right now, I couldn't solve any problem. Not even two plus two. I'm just too tired. Sleep! It's only eight-thirty, but I can't stay awake a second longer. I haven't even got the energy to take my clothes off. If anything keeps me up for a sec — no, even half a second longer — they will have to take me to the hospital for the critically exhausted. The supermarket newspapers will put my picture on the front page:

ELEVEN-YEAR-OLD IN CRITICAL
CONDITION FROM TOO MUCH FUN.

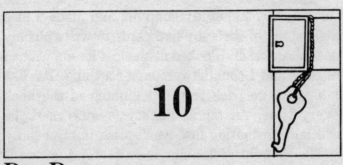

10

Dear **D**iary:

Thursday afternoon. Cold and blustery.

I stayed home from school today. I have the flu. Darcy got it first and then Baby Rose. Mom and Dad had it at the same time and now me.

I feel like I'm going to die, but I realize I probably won't. Mom brought the little black-and-white TV into my room and put it up on the dresser and said I could just watch the soaps and not to worry about homework until I was feeling better, but I *have* to worry.

I am going to flunk history. Mr. Burrows told me as much the other day. It was so embarrassing. When he told me I started to cry. He said maybe if I got an A on the big test and did a *spectacular* extra-credit project I could pull myself back into the passing range. But I could see from the look on his face that, as much as he likes me, Mr. Burrows does not think I'm going to get it together enough to pass history.

I got out the history book, opened it on my desk,

turned the little study lamp on, and made a nice little stack of three-by-five cards to write out my dates. And then I looked at the last lesson we had in class and I couldn't remember a thing. It's like I have to go back to the beginning of the book every time. As far as history is concerned the crucial information just won't stick in my head.

The thought of flunking is *so* depressing that it weighs on me all the time. Although I've goofed off in the past, I've never actually failed a subject. It would be a first, and *not* a first I'm looking forward to. My parents will be so upset if I fail. And what about Gram, who thinks I'm practically perfect? I just can't stand thinking of disappointing them. And that's why, even though I was so bleary-eyed I could hardly read a comic book, I was trying to study history in bed. Not that I was getting anything accomplished. Once the book fell off the bed while I was sleeping and I picked it up at a different page and got the idea that Abraham Lincoln was a friend of George Washington.

Around noon, Josh came home from school. Looks like *he's* got this flu now, too. He dragged by, looking miserable, then dragged back again, then inched in and took a few of my Kleenexes. He also told me he's in love. Sometimes, after weeks of acting like I'm just too young and stupid to bother with, Josh will make the most astounding announcements, tell me the most private stuff about himself.

·I asked him with who, and he said Mary Lou Witty. She's a senior, the head of the cheerleading squad. She's in love with some college guy and acts like Josh is kind of a pal, a tagalong little brother. Which just kills him. Life is so weird. Josh could probably have ninety-nine percent of the girls at his school for a girlfriend. So who does he fall in love with? One of the one percent that isn't interested in him.

I told him to start ignoring her a little. This always seems to work for the characters on the soaps. As soon as anyone loses interest in someone else, that person goes nuts and starts chasing them. He said he'd think about it. Then he realized he was having an actual discussion with his kid sister, and got up and said he was going to take a nap before Adam got home and woke him up with his boom box.

I wonder what it would be like to be in love. I just can't imagine it. Especially not with any of the boys at Claremont. They just seem like such a hopeless collection. Boys *must* be better at other schools. Ours are either bullies or wimps or weirdos — and I mean from the Planet Zorg!

Everyone, well Mom and Dad and Josh and Mrs. Freed, the family studies teacher, says this will all change suddenly. One day I'll hit puberty and — shazam! — one of these mutants will turn into Prince Charming and sweep me off my feet.

Frankly, I have a little trouble believing this. But there's a big dance at the end of sixth grade, which means I'm supposed to be at least a little interested in boys by the end of this school year. And interested *specifically* in the boys who go to Claremont. Doubtsies. I know them all too well, from their even more hideous days, fourth and fifth grade. If I got interested, it would have to be in somebody a little more mysterious.

Oh, I suppose I might fall in love with a boy in my class if the sixth grade went on a field trip on a ship and we all got shipwrecked on a desert island, and there was no hope of ever meeting anyone else. Maybe after years and years (with my judgment affected by being out in the sun too long and eating only coconuts and fish), I might be able to be interested in Billy Watts. He's at least nicer than the others.

But really, even if they were more interesting, I don't have time to be chasing after boys. I am already behind in my whole life. Beginning with history.

Gram brought me lunch on a little tray. She is so nice to me. I ate the cup of soup and a chicken sandwich and a big glass of orange juice. Then she took my history book and put it on my book-shelf ("just for today") and stayed to watch *The Young and the Restless* with me.

I told her all about my weekend in Detroit, and about Nancy's problem with her father.

"She needs her father's attention," I explained.

"No," Gram said. "She has his attention. No girl could be getting more attention. What she needs is to know he's listening to her."

"You're right," I said. "That's exactly the problem." Gram always hits the nail on the head when it comes to personal problems.

She sat there next to my bed for a while, thinking hard about Nancy, then said, "When you want to tell somebody something that's hard to tell them, you have to think of the most positive way to put it. It's often just a question of emphasis. Like in this case, Nancy should emphasize that what she wants to do is spend more time *talking* to her dad, and that all the activities are kind of standing in the way. If she puts it like this, her dad should see that she cares more about *him* than about all the plays and restaurants. My guess is he'll be flattered."

"You're so wise," I told her. She blushed. It's hard to believe grandmothers can still blush. I guess there's still a little bit of girl left in them. When I'm older, I want to be just like Gram. She's very cool for her age. She doesn't even have gray hair. She dyes it. It's supposed to be a secret, but I went to the beauty shop with her once, so I know. But I probably won't be like her when I'm her age. Given how I am now, I will probably be a very crabby old person and yell at kids who come on my lawn. And I'll have lots of gray (probably frizzy) hair from all the worrying I'll have been doing since way back when I flunked history.

11

Dear **D**iary:

Tonight I went up to ask Mom if I could have a slumber party. I was in knots hoping she'd say yes. I just know the party is my big chance to get into the cool crowd.

When I found her, Mom was stretched across the bed, lying on her stomach, reading a magazine. I hated to interrupt her in what was probably her one moment of peace in the day. But if I didn't talk to her now, next thing I knew she'd be in the middle of something, too busy or frantic or preoccupied to pay attention to this important question.

She looked up and patted the bed to show me I should come over and sit down.

"Can I ask you something?"

"Sure. Always. What's on your mind?" Even when she's resting, Mom still talks a mile a minute.

"Oh, I don't know. I was just kind of thinking. Well, you know . . . that I'd like to have a slumber party."

79

"You mean have Nancy sleep over?"

"Well, sure, Nancy. But a few other girls, too. I don't know. Maybe Samantha and Candace."

"I thought you hated Samantha with a passion," Mom said.

"Well, I do. But I'm hating her less lately. She's being nice to me. Actually the party was kind of her idea."

"Why doesn't she have her *own* slumber party?"

"I don't know. She just thought it would be neat if I did," I answered.

I could see my mother had some reservations about this. She probably didn't trust Samantha. Now I was sorry I'd told her so many rotten things about Samantha in the past. It was going to be hard to show that Samantha had changed.

"Lizzie," my mother said now. "I don't want to offend you, but do you think it's possible Samantha has some hidden reason for wanting to be friends with you?"

"Mom! That's just what Nancy thinks. Why is it that no one believes anyone could just want to be my friend for my own sake!?"

"Oh, honey. I'm sorry. That's not what I was trying to say. It doesn't have anything to do with you. It's just that Samantha is such a tricky person. Forget it. I'm probably just being overprotective. You know us mothers."

"Uh, Mom?" I put in, in case she forgot the point of this talk.

"Yes?"

"About the slumber party . . ."

"Oh, right. Couldn't you make it a tea party instead? I won't get a wink of sleep that night."

"Tea party? Moth — er! I promise we'll all be really quiet and go right to sleep."

"Lizzie. I remember slumber parties, and nobody is ever quiet at them, and nobody ever goes to sleep! Maybe you could have a brunch."

"Mom! Grade-school kids don't have brunches." I was getting nervous.

"Well, I suppose if you're dying to do this, I can give up one night's sleep."

"Oh, Mom!" I shouted, leaping up and giving her a big hug.

"Now wait just one more second," she said. "I don't want this taking over your life. It's only a party. I want to see you taking care of the important things first — your piano lessons, your schoolwork. I want to see good grades on your mid-term report card, or there aren't going to be *any* parties around here."

"Oh," I said.

"Is that going to be a problem?" she asked, looking suspicious. I hadn't mentioned the troubles I was having in history.

"Oh, no. No problem. No problem at all."

I gave Mom another hug and walked out of the room and down the hall, muttering "No problem" to myself. I mean, how was I ever going to get a decent grade in history?

I was deep in despair. Just when I was on the brink of popularity, one slumber party away, I was going to be foiled by history. By George Washington and Dolley Madison and Ben Franklin. A bunch of dead people who couldn't care less about my slumber party. It didn't seem fair. I didn't stand in the way of the American Revolution. Why should *it* stand in the way of my social success?

Then I got this great flash. I'd get Nancy to help me!

This will be tricky, though. The main reason I need her help is to pass history so I can have a party she's sure to think is the stupidest social event in the world. Plus, she'll probably be insulted when she figures out the party is to please Samantha.

Boy, there are so many things I can't talk to Nancy about these days. The party. Samantha. My lipstick. I haven't even told *you* about my lipstick. I got it the other day at Singer's Drugs. It's not really lipstick, it's called Lip Enhancer. It's a shade called "Nude," which means you can hardly tell you've got it on. That is, Mom and Dad and the teachers at school can't tell I've got it on. But I can, and it really does make me look different. In a subtle way. More sophisticated. More like a Liz than a Lizzie.

Nancy would say Lip Enhancer was just a total rip-off. Of course, Nancy's idea of high fashion is having both shoelaces in your sneakers the same color.

We are just poles apart these days. This past week we haven't even gone to school together. She insists on riding her bike while I want to walk now. She says this is just stupid, that by bike it takes half as long. But you really can't ride a bike wearing a skirt, and I find I'm wearing more skirts to school.

Nancy wouldn't be caught dead in a skirt. She's still a tomboy. She actually climbed a tree Saturday when we were on our way home from playing tennis. I got embarrassed in case anyone was around and saw her. She saw that I was embarrassed and got hurt.

She can't understand why I care about being popular. Actually, I'm not sure why myself. But I know I care. I know I'd like to have tons of friends calling me every night, and get invited to other kids' houses, and to their parties. I'd like to be noticed around school. I would like people to think my jokes are incredibly funny, and that I'm smart in class without being a show-off about it.

I'd like people to say, "Oh that Lizzie Miletti —
of course, her really close friends, all one hundred
of them, call her Liz. . . ." Stuff like that.

Nancy doesn't care a bit about popularity. Her
big thing lately is that she wants to build a tree
house.

But that's the thing about Nancy. Even though
she's off-and-on mad at me these days, and even
if she knows I'm only getting her help so I can
have a party she thinks is stupid to impress a
bunch of girls she hates — even then she'll help
me with my history if I ask her. Why? Because
whatever differences we may have, Nancy is my
best friend.

12

Dear **D**iary:

Today in history Mr. Burrows reminded us all that the history test is in just a week. And that all extra-credit projects are due the same day.

"I'm sure most of you will do just fine," he said. "The grades in this class have been quite high, I must say. And those few of you who haven't been trying hard enough . . ."

He paused here and gave me the fishy eye.

" . . . I'm sure you've been busy catching up and will surprise me."

I felt my ears starting to burn as he said this. I knew I hadn't been catching up at all. If anything, I've been falling even farther behind. How could I have let things slide so badly? All week I meant to really crack down. But something always came up.

Sunday, I was still getting over the flu. On Monday, Chester, Adam's geriatric hamster, had died, and we threw him a funeral. Adam read a little poem:

"He was a great hamster
Loved his crunchy meal.
Spent a lot of time.
Goin' round in his wheel."

And then we put the little box, with Chester in it, into a hole in the big field beyond the backyard.

Tuesday I had a book report due on a biography of Amelia Earhart. Wednesday I went over to Cusmano's Tuxedo Rental to look at the dinner jacket Josh was renting. He's taking Mary Lou Witty to the Fall Fantasia dance at Hampton Point High. He can't believe she said yes. It's a good thing I went to Cusmano's with him. He'd picked the grossest jacket — pink with black piping. I talked him into a plain blue.

Anyway, it was already Thursday and the test was next Thursday. Not only hadn't I studied, but I didn't have an extra-credit project done. Or even started. Actually, I didn't even have an *idea* for a project.

I was going to *have* to ask Nancy for help. I'd been putting this off because she was sure to give me a lecture. I could just hear her say, "Lizzie — how did you let yourself get into this mess?"

And sure enough, when I'd caught up with her at the bike rack after school and poured out my sad story about flunking history and needing to pass in order to have my slumber party, the first thing Nancy said was, "Lizzie — how did you let yourself get into this mess?"

I started rattling off a list of really good excuses, but she just put up her hand to stop me.

"I don't want to hear all this. It doesn't matter anyway. You're clearly the grasshopper — not giving a thought to tomorrow. While I am the ant — dutifully storing up for the long winter ahead."

"Okay, okay," I said. "But you *will* help me, won't you? Even though I'm such a grasshopper?"

Nancy sighed, squeezed the hand brakes on her bike, and rolled her eyes around to show how exasperated she was with me.

"Oh, of course I will. That's the kind of animals we ants are. That's why we make such good friends. Unlike some other animals. Snakes, for instance."

This, I knew, was a subtle reference to Samantha. I didn't say anything. I didn't want to bring up that subject today. I'd already had to bring up the slumber party, which was one touchy subject too many.

"Will you come home from school with me?" I asked Nancy. "I need to start right away. Actually, I need to start three weeks ago."

Nancy nodded. "I'll call my mom when she gets home from work. We need to get over to the library."

Nancy's mom is a computer programmer. That really impresses me.

"But I can study at home," I said.

"We'll study later. First we need to get you started on your extra-credit project. The way you've been going you're going to need every bit of extra credit you can get. We have to go to the library and start your research."

I nodded as though I knew what she was talking about, then I looked up with a big question mark in my head. "Uh, just what *is* my project?"

"The project I didn't do when I decided to build my replica of the Mayflower instead. This other project's a great idea, though."

"I can't wait to hear," I said gloomily. To me, projects just mean tons of work. Plus, I'm terrible at them. Even after all my work, my projects always turn out terribly.

"A big chart of all the American Indian tribes. We can put pictures on it and samples of their costumes. And little signs for whether they were hunters or gatherers. That sort of thing."

"A peace pipe or two," I said.

"This is no laughing matter, Lizzie Miletti. You have gotten yourself into big trouble, and it's going to take all my help and all your hard work to bail you out."

"Oh, all right," I said, and sighed. "Let's go."

But Nancy didn't get back on her bike right away. Instead, she started fidgeting, hopping a little from one foot to the other. This was a sure sign she was nervous about something. I waited to find out what this something was.

"Here," she finally said, pulling an envelope from the back pocket of her jeans. "Now *you* can help *me* for a minute. Read this and tell me what you think."

It was a letter to her dad.

> *Dear Dad,*
> *I was really looking forward to coming down to visit again next weekend, but it looks like I won't be able to come now. The problem is that I've broken my leg . . .*

I stopped reading and looked at her in amazement.

"No. N-O!" I said. "That's ridiculous! You can't start faking major injuries. This is too weird. I think you've just got to find some way to talk to your dad about how freaked-out you're getting."

"I can't. Not after all the trouble he's been going

to. It'll look like I don't appreciate any of it," Nancy said, starting to cry.

"Well, how do you think your sulking and silence makes him feel? Nancy, I think you just have to start telling your true feelings to him. You've got to let him know who you are. Whether you like it or not, we *are* changing . . ."

I paused here, afraid Nancy would get mad at my touching on this sensitive subject, but she just kept looking at me, listening really seriously. So I went on.

" . . . and your dad's been away from your regular life for a couple of years now. He doesn't really know you any more. You've got to talk to him. I can *see* he loves you. Maybe all the activities are his way of trying to find some things the two of you can share. He can't be the couch-potato dad for you anymore, just hanging around the house. And I think he can't figure out what other kind of dad he *can* be. You've got to help him. Otherwise you're going to be sixty and he's going to be ninety, and he'll be taking you to the Ice Capades and you'll be sitting there, miserable and silent."

Nancy nodded, like she was taking all this in.

"You're right. I can see you're right. But I can't seem to do it. When I start to say something real to him, it gets all stuck inside me. It's like shyness, only worse. And more complicated."

"What are the complications?" I asked her.

Nancy shook her head.

"I'm not sure. I think part of it is that I'm really mad at him for not being around anymore. I guess I think he's showing me all these great times because he feels bad for leaving Mom and me."

"Then tell him. I think he'll understand. And then you two can have a new beginning."

There were big tears in Nancy's eyes as she leaned across the bike rack to give me a hug. Not a noogie, but a *hug*.

"I know you're right. Now I just have to find a way to be able to say these things to him. See why I don't want to grow up? It's just so hard."

"But at least when you grow up, you won't have to do history projects," I said, grinning.

Nancy gave me a light noogie on the head and said, "We'd better get going. We've got a lot of work to do. Research, research, research. Then over to MacDermott's for construction paper and paste and . . ." In the middle of this, Nancy started looking at me more closely and then finally asked, "Have you got stuff on your lips?"

"Uh, not really," I said, but I was secretly smiling. Clearly, the Lip Enhancer was looking subtly great.

"Hmmm," Nancy said. "They look kind of weird. Maybe you ought to go see a doctor. I think you might be getting that flu back."

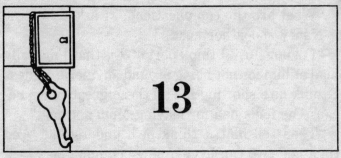

13

Dear **D**iary:

Nancy came over to help me with my history project again tonight, but I could tell her heart wasn't in it.

When she threw a handful of feathers into the air and said, "Comanche? Apache? — who cares?" I said, "Hey, Nance — what's the matter?"

"Nothing," she said. But I know that "nothing," so I just kept looking hard at her until she gave in and told me.

"I'm supposed to go see my dad this weekend and I'm just dreading it."

"Didn't you call him today?" I said. I was a little miffed that she hadn't taken my great advice.

"I've just been too chicken, I guess. I don't think I can do it."

"Sure you can."

"No. I can't."

"You can. With my help."

"How can you help me make a phone call?" she said.

"Just wait and see. Stay here and try to make a passable tomahawk for the Blackfoot display, and I'll be right back."

I rushed out, then stuck my head back in the doorway and said, "Trust me."

I knew just what I was going to do. I got my biggest felt-tip marker and went up to my parents' bedroom and dug around in my dad's shirt drawer. He keeps the old cardboards from the laundry there in case we kids need them. When there are five kids in a house, somebody always needs cardboard for one project or another. Luckily there was a big supply tonight. I sat down on the floor and got right to work.

In fifteen minutes I was done and back up in my room. Nancy looked up. She had a feather stuck to her cheek and looked pretty funny.

"What've you done?" she asked, trying to get a look at my cardboard pieces.

"Just what they do for Johnny Carson and the President of the United States — I made cue cards for your whole conversation with your dad. All you have to do is dial his number, I'll hold them up, and from there on it'll be a breeze."

This idea seemed to make her nervous.

"Uh, do you think you could kind of read the cards to me as I go along instead? I . . . uh, kind of have trouble reading when I'm uptight."

"Sure. I'll just whisper in your ear as you go along. Like a prompter in a play."

She grinned. "Lizzie, sometimes I truly think you're a genius. Now can I see the brilliant script you've written for me?"

She looked over the cards, reading slowly, crossing out a few things she didn't think she could say, laughing when she came to one on which I'd written, "And Dad, could you please buy Lizzie a compact disc player? She's such a wonderful person."

When we were all set, we went to the phone in the hallway, and she dialed her dad's number.

"Uh, hi, Dad," she started. So far so good.

He said hi back, just as I planned for in my cards.

"About this weekend . . ." I told her to say, and she repeated it.

As I predicted, her dad rushed in with this long list of stuff he had planned for them to do when she got there. I whispered into her ear my next line, and she repeated it to her dad.

"Well, what I was thinking was — just for a change — it would really be nice to spend a little downtime together. Maybe rent a video. Order in a pizza. Read a book. You know. Just hang out."

Then her dad said, "But I've already bought tickets to this musical downtown for Saturday, and I've made reservations at a Japanese steak house for Friday."

I hadn't planned on this, and so my next card, which said, "Great, I'm glad you agree," didn't fit the conversation at all anymore, so I had to drop the cards and make something up.

I whispered in Nancy's ear. "Dad, the thing is . . . I sort of twisted my ankle."

Nancy repeated this into the phone without thinking and then, realizing what she was saying, she looked at me with her eyes widening. I limped around the room, pointing at my "twisted" ankle, and then I sat down in a chair and took a book. I pretended to read. I shut my eyes. I rested. I couldn't believe I had done it. I mean, I was encouraging Nancy to make up this whole story for her father.

Nancy caught on right away. "Dad," she said quickly. "It's nothing serious. I just can't run around much. You know, I have to take it easy."

I listened to Nancy and had to be impressed by how she was throwing herself into this thing. When she said, "Fine, Dad. So we'll just hang out at home most of the weekend," I silently clapped my hands at Nancy.

When Nancy hung up, she said, "No faking major injuries . . . isn't that what you said?"

"Right," I agreed. "I don't know what came over me, but a twisted ankle is only a *minor* injury. It's not a broken leg."

Nancy shook her head sadly. "Okay, so this is great for one weekend, but it really leaves me in the same place."

"Not really," I said eagerly. "While you're having your quiet weekend, you can tell him how much you are enjoying it. Maybe he'll get the hint. You'll have enough quiet time to tell him all the things we've talked about. You'll see."

Nancy looked doubtful. "If I can get my courage up," she said.

"He's your father, Nancy," I said. "He's not a stranger."

Nancy shrugged. "Sometimes he feels like a stranger lately. You wouldn't know because your father is here all the time."

I suddenly felt lucky. In spite of colored string beans and all the other junk I had to eat, my dad was with me every day.

"Okay," Nancy said, standing up. "We have masses of work to do on your chart. Tell me the truth, does this look like a tomahawk?" She held up some strange object.

"I thought it was a peace pipe," I told her. "Either one is okay. So just stick it on."

Well, we got the chart almost half done, but there's still so much more to do. And then there is studying for the test. I'm never going to pass. I'm going to fail in spite of Nancy's help. I just know it. What should I do, Diary?

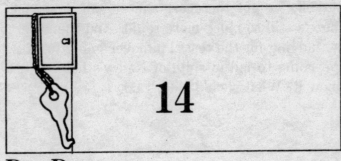

14

Dear **D**iary:

What a week! I haven't had a chance to write a single line to you, because Nancy has been like an army drill sergeant in the movies. She comes home with me after school every day and just makes me study, study, study. Mom came in the room during one of those sessions, and, seeing my terrified face, asked, "What is going on here?"

I hadn't told her about how badly I was doing. I just couldn't think about how awful she'd feel, but there was no point in hiding it anymore, so I confessed. "But, Nancy, my coach, is going to get me through. I know I'll pass." I tried to sound confident."

My mother looked really upset. "How could you not tell me something so important, Lizzie? I would have gotten you a tutor. Or I would have helped you myself. Don't you trust me?"

I guess I must have looked more miserable than ever, so Mom quickly gave me a hug and patted Nancy on the shoulder. But before she left the room she looked at both of us and said, "If you fail *any* subject, Lizzie, there is no slumber party in your immediate future." My mom can be very tough when she wants to be.

Nancy and I bore down even harder. Every minute we weren't in school, she was tutoring me. I had to pass.

Names, dates, places, battles, inventions. She made flash cards for all of them. She made me highlight every chapter in my book in one color, then go back and highlight all the next most important stuff in another color.

I don't know how she knows all this stuff. The funny thing is that I almost never see her reading. It's like she's got it all memorized or something.

Whenever I'd get too punchy from answering questions or reciting dates, we'd take a break — to work on my Indian tribes chart. Some break! More little tom-toms, more feathers on the tribal locations. More little tomahawks or baskets to show whether the tribes were hunters or gatherers. Nancy was a big help on this, though. She even broke open a string of her beads so we could glue them on the chart as trading beads. We'd work on the chart together until our fingers stuck together with glue, and our hair was full of feathers. By Tuesday the map was done. And because of Nancy's help — she's not that artistic, but she's *very* careful — it looked a whole lot better than my usual projects.

Then on Wednesday night she stayed up all night with me. By this time, we were through Columbus and the pilgrims and the thirteen colonies, and Nancy was trying to drum the American Revolution through my thick skull. And thick it is.

It was about eleven, I think, when Nancy said something about some King George, and I said, "Who's he?"

She looked at me in this kind of insane way, her eyes getting larger, like a mad scientist. I thought I'd take a wild guess and try to calm her down.

"Oh yeah — King George. Didn't he have something to do with the Civil War?"

At this point she lunged and began strangling me.

"Wrong, huh? You should just give up on me," I said in despair. "I'm a hopeless case."

But she wouldn't have it. "After all the work I've put in on you?!" she said. "No way! When the going gets tough . . ."

". . . I go to sleep," I said, climbing up into my bed and pulling the pillow over my head. I just wanted to escape.

But Nancy yanked it right off again and made me sit down and started over again. I don't know how long she drilled me, how many thousands of questions she asked me before we finally just dropped in our tracks and fell asleep.

The morning of the test, I was totally exhausted. The questions swam around in front of my eyes. I felt like the confused contestant on some TV quiz show where I wasn't quite sure of the rules.

But somehow I finished. A lot ahead of the others, which scared me. Maybe I hadn't given the questions enough thought. But it was all the thought I had, so I just got up and turned in my paper to Mr. Burrows.

Of course, as soon as I did that, I regretted it. I thought I should have gone over my answers. And then I really got nervous when the other kids started coming out into the hallway saying how tough they thought the test was. I worried all of Friday and then over the weekend, too. Nancy was in Detroit, so I didn't have her to talk to about all my worries. Probably just as well. I would have driven her crazy. It wasn't the slumber party anymore. I wanted to pass because I didn't want Lizzie Miletti to fail anything.

On Monday Mr. Burrows handed the tests back. I held my breath as he started alphabetically with Patty Adams and Ted Cahill and so on. I crossed my fingers on both hands and shut my eyes until I felt a piece of paper fluttering down in front of my face onto the desk. I opened my eyes and looked down.

I couldn't believe it when I saw the C at the top of my test paper. Neither could Mr. Burrows, although underneath his look of amazement I thought I could see a happy look.

Mom and Dad were happy, too, and relieved. Mom said now I could go ahead and plan my slumber party.

I really owed Nancy one. I told her I'd take her out on Saturday — today — anywhere she wanted. She said I should pick.

I know she likes Tom Cruise, so I took her to the theaters out at the mall where his new movie is playing. We sat through it twice, it was so good. Then I took her over to the Zephyr. Nancy especially likes their peanut-butter sundae. I myself prefer the traditional banana split.

Well, it was a terrific afternoon — like the old times we used to have together. Best friends stuff. Movies and riding our bikes and pigging out on ice cream. When we'd been there a while, Samantha and Candace and Jessica Aldridge came in and took a booth by the window.

Not that they eat ice cream. They were just there to have diet drinks and see what boys showed up. Some boys from our class were there. Robert Wilkins. Louis Burke. Alan Maggio. Dave Price. Not Billy Watts. I might have waved and said hi to him. A bigger group of mutant proto-plasm you've never seen. But Samantha and Candace were acting like they were fascinating creatures. In spite of the fact that all they could do was shoot their straw wrappers across the room at Candace and Samantha and Jessica. They didn't bother shooting wrappers at me and Nancy. They know we think they're mutants. But you know, I wouldn't have minded if one of them *had* shot a straw wrapper at me. Not that I'd ever tell Nancy.

I wanted to invite Samantha and her friends to my slumber party, now that I was officially having it. I waited until we were done eating our sundaes. I didn't want to upset Nancy, since it was her treat afternoon. But then when she went to the ladies' room, I kind of casually went over to the booth where Samantha and her friends were sitting.

"Oh, hi, Liz," Samantha said. "What's up?" She was warm and friendly.

I got so nervous I started stuttering. "I-I-I just wanted to invite you all to my slumber party."

"Oh, great!" Samantha said and flashed this look at the others like they should think it was great, too, and eventually they smiled and looked interested.

"Well, when is this big bash?" Samantha asked me, smiling the way you do at a good friend.

I said it was Friday night and that even though it was just before Halloween, nobody had to wear a costume.

The three of them laughed in this pukey way, kind of a phony chuckle, and Candace said, "You mean we're not going to go trick-or-treating?"

I didn't say anything. The fact is that Nancy and I *were* planning to go trick-or-treating. We thought we'd get one good last year in before we were too old. I didn't mention this to the Cool Ones, though. They just would have looked down their noses at me.

Then, out of the corner of my eye, I saw Nancy coming out of the ladies' room in the back, so I rushed to finish this conversation. "So come around seven on Friday, okay? You won't forget?"

"I *couldn't* forget," Samantha said sweetly. "I wouldn't miss your party."

"Who else is coming?" Candace asked me.

"Uh, I don't know. I guess I haven't really thought about it much yet. You're the first people I've invited."

Apparently my mom *had* thought about who I should invite, though. As soon as I got home, she asked me to come down to the laundry room and help her fold wash for a while. This usually means she has something she wants to talk with me about. The laundry room is down in the basement and it's usually a place where you can have a private conversation.

"Just who's coming to this party?" she asked me when we'd pulled a load of towels out of the dryer.

"Well, Nancy and me. And today I invited Samantha and Candace and Jessica Aldridge."

"What about the other girls in the class?"

I told her these were about the only ones I thought would be fun.

"What about Polly Hart and that Tanya, and Diane Easton? She just lives down the street. You don't want to exclude them."

I didn't know how to talk about this. I didn't want to say that Tanya and Diane and Polly were the Supernerds, that Samantha and her friends would never hang out with them in a million years. I tried to describe how weird the nerds were, without exactly calling them that.

I told her how Tanya ate her stupid beets every day and how Diane wore a trenchcoat at gym, and how I didn't think they'd fit in at my party. I said Polly would probably bring along a report on the history of slumber parties. Something stupid and embarrassing.

I thought I was making a pretty good case, but Mom just got this more and more serious look on her face. Finally she told me I was going to have to invite all the girls in the class or none of them.

"I've watched how you hated being excluded by Samantha and her crowd. And you should think about how these other girls would feel if you did the same thing to them."

I kind of saw what she meant. Everyone would hear about the party. And anyone not invited would for sure feel left out. Still, I couldn't imagine all the girls in my class actually having fun together in our family room. I told Mom this.

"Well, maybe they won't. Maybe they'll break down into the same groups they do in school. Maybe you'll wind up having several little parties instead of one big one. But you'll be able to feel you did the right thing. Which is more important than being popular."

I nodded, to show her I was taking her seriously. I went upstairs feeling extremely noble and virtuous. Like Mother Teresa, only on a smaller scale. But I still couldn't imagine anyone having fun at this party I'm now stuck with having. And I feel my mom certainly didn't understand sixth-grade social life.

How did I get into this mess?!

15

Dear Diary:

It's Saturday night and I'm all alone up in my room. Thinking about my party last night. And about Nancy. And Samantha. And the nerds. And where I went wrong.

Everything started okay, except that I was *so* nervous. I got home from school and immediately started getting ready. The first step was Miletti-proofing my party. I talked to Darcy and Baby Rose about not making nuisances of themselves at my party, and they agreed . . . sulking a lot.

Then I found Josh and Adam shooting baskets in the driveway and as tactfully as possible, told them the same thing.

"Mary Lou Witty has decided she can't wait until the dance to go out with me," Josh said smugly. "So I'm not even going to be home tonight."

"Me either," Adam said. "I'm going to a concert in Detroit, then staying over at Eric's."

Great, I thought. That took care of all the siblings. Gram and Mom would never do anything to disrupt the party. And I wasn't even sure Dad would be back home by tonight. He'd been away all week at the company headquarters. Meetings about some big new Roth product.

After I talked to everyone in my family, I took a shower, got dressed, and started setting up the party in the family room. Even though the party was to celebrate my new bedroom, that was way too small a space to hold all my guests. I sat down on the sofa and counted up just how many of them were coming.

Nancy, of course. Well, I say "of course," but for a while I wasn't sure she would come. When I invited her, she said she'd have to think about it. That's Nancy.

Then there were Samantha and Candace and Jessica. And, on the other end of the social plan — all three of the Supernerds. Tanya, Diane, and Polly had all said yes to my invitation. Oh, and Ericka Powell, the new girl, was coming too. That made nine. More people than I'd ever had over at once. More people by eight, since I'd really only had Nancy over. I was lucky some of the girls in my class couldn't come.

I was nervous just thinking of all the possible things that could go wrong. Finally I just made myself stop thinking and started putting pretzels into little bowls. Then I went upstairs and changed my outfit. Then I changed it three more times. Finally I decided on blue jeans and a pale blue long-sleeved turtleneck. Very casual. And if I didn't feel like changing into pajamas later, I could even *sleep* in this outfit.

By six-thirty I was completely ready. I sat down in the family room and looked around. Chips and pretzels. A washtub filled with ice and cans of soda. I'd added a Halloween touch with a jack-o-lantern on top of the TV. I'd brought down my boom box and stack of tapes. Mom had helped me push the sofa and recliner back against the wall so we'd have room for everyone to roll out their sleeping bags.

Checklist complete, I remember thinking. And then the doorbell rang. It was Nancy. I'd asked her to get here early so I'd have someone to be nervous with. *She* wasn't nervous at all. She didn't even seem excited to be at my party. She hadn't dressed up at all. She was just wearing on old pair of jeans and a sweatshirt with paint smears on it. She'd brought a sleeping bag and half a box of snack mix.

The first thing she said was did I want to play some Super Mario Brothers with her, and then didn't even wait for me to answer — just went over to the TV set and put the cartridge in. I thought we should be listening to tapes and snacking and relaxing on the sofa when the others

arrived. I thought that would look more sophisticated. But I knew I'd just sound stupid
trying to explain this to Nancy, so I let her play
the video game.

At 7:01, no one else had shown up, and I sunk
into the pits. No one was going to come to my
party, I was just sure of it. But then at 7:02 the
bell rang. It was Ericka Powell and her dad.
They'd brought both a sleeping bag and a big
tent.

"We thought it might be fun," Ericka said,
meaning the tent. "This kind doesn't need stakes.
You can just set it up on the floor."

She showed me and Nancy how it worked, and
we all put it together. It gave us a chance to get
to know each other, too. I finally asked Ericka the
questions I'd had on my mind at the beginning of
the school year. Did she ever live in an igloo? Did
she know any Eskimos? Did she ever pan for gold?

No, yes, no were the answers, but the questions
made her laugh. She said it was like being inter-
viewed by Barbara Walters.

I liked Ericka a lot, and I could tell Nancy did,
too. So far, the party was going great. But then
the doorbell rang again, and there was Tanya Malone, with no sleeping bag. I just knew someone
would forget hers, and I'd have to lend out mine.
What she did have with her was a big freezer
carton.

"Party beets," she told me.

I took the carton and told her I'd serve them later. To myself I said — *much* later, maybe next Tuesday.

I got Tanya a can of soda, but then I didn't know what else to do, so I just let her sit on the sofa, looking nervous and scared. And then the doorbell rang again, and I couldn't worry about her anymore.

This time it was Polly and Diane. They'd brought a mountain of things with them. It looked like they were planning to stay a week. They had sleeping bags and duffels and a grocery bag full of snack stuff.

I helped them unpack everything and then didn't know what they wanted to do, so I asked them.

"I think we'd like to knit for a while if that's all right," Polly said.

Knit? I thought. At a *party*? I couldn't believe my eyes as they went over to the sofa, sat down next to Tanya, and pulled out these horrendous multi-colored socks, and began clicking away like elves in a knitting workshop. I looked around to see what Nancy thought about this, but she was already absorbed in playing Super Mario Brothers with Ericka.

When the doorbell rang the next time, I knew it had to be Samantha and her friends. They were the only ones who'd really dressed up for the party. Samantha was wearing black stretch pants with an oversized red sweatshirt. The outfit really showed off her great blonde looks. Candace was a contrast in a slouchy seafoam-green cotton sweater and perfectly faded jeans. Jessica, who's a redhead, was wearing baby-blue designer sweats. All together, the three of them looked like a group of models who'd just shown up for a fashion photography shoot.

I wished my party was at a more fun stage. I could see how it must look to them. Although there were quite a few girls there now, nobody had really gotten together. Nothing *partyish* was happening. It looked more like a waiting room in a bus station.

I heard Candace saying something in a low voice to Samantha.

"*Tons* of fun." She said this sarcastically, and it made me wish a little trapdoor would open up underneath me and swallow me up. Then I wouldn't have to be here at this terrible party. *My* party. But Samantha told Candace to keep quiet, and I felt very grateful to her.

It was about then that the party went from terrible dull to terrible weird. The kitchen door swung open, and my dad was suddenly in the room holding this tray of peculiar-looking popsicles. I didn't even know he'd come home.

"Girls," he said in his salesman's voice, "when you came here tonight, you thought you were just going to an ordinary slumber party. Little did you realize you were going to be part of American marketing history!"

Oh no, I thought to myself. How could he? I knew right off that these weren't any regular popsicles. They were some new Roth frozen product. I watched my guests bite into theirs, and then watched their expressions change dramatically.

"Uh, Mr. Miletti," Polly asked, "just what is this unusual . . . uh . . . flavor?

And my dad said, "Well, you've got a green one, so it's got to be either spinach or broccoli."

"Spin . . .?"

"Yes, lucky ladies," my dad boomed, "what you're eating are the very first prototypes of America's newest snack concept — Vegicles!"

I remember thinking, This is the low point of my life. My party was going down the tubes!

I grabbed Nancy and took her into a corner. "I want to leave," I said.

"You can't leave. It's your party." she said smugly. "I knew this wasn't going to work."

"I'll never be able to hold my head up in this town, ever."

Now Nancy softened for a moment. "Don't be a jerk. It's only one night. Don't worry. Come over and get into the who-can-blow-the-biggest-bubble contest with me and Ericka."

See what I mean about Nancy? I didn't want to do anything that childish in front of Samantha and Candace and Jessica. "Maybe a little later," I told Nancy, stalling for time.

Samantha and Candace and Jessica had put a tape on the boom box and were dancing in the far corner of the family room, on the other side of the tent — kind of having a little party of their own. I went over, not sure of what to say to them.

"Come on and dance with us," Samantha said, pulling me into their circle.

"Uh . . . well . . ." I started to expain that I didn't really know how to dance. But she said I had to start sometime and with the sixth-grade dance at the end of the school year coming up, I might as well start now. So I sort of hopped around imitating Samantha, and it seemed to work.

"You're good," she shouted to me after a while.

I blushed like crazy, but then I added a few steps to my great dancing method, along with a little thing I did with my hands. I was really getting into it.

A couple of times I looked across the room and saw Nancy and Ericka blowing giant bubble-gum bubbles. Polly and Diane were still knitting. Tanya Malone was just sitting inside the tent by herself. I could see her through the little screen flap and felt guilty for a second. I thought I probably ought to go and do something to be a good hostess. Maybe ask if she wanted to serve her party beets now. But then I just got absorbed in my dancing, which was getting better by the minute.

Then I saw Nancy coming over to ask me something. She ignored Samantha and her friends entirely and just stood next to me until I turned down the tape so I could hear her.

"Ericka and I were thinking it might be fun to play a game of hide-and-go-seek. Just to be silly."

At first I thought she was kidding. Then, when I saw she was serious, I almost died. How juvenile! And with Samantha and Candace and Jessica all standing there, listening. How was I going to handle this?

"Uh, well . . . that sounds great," I mumbled to Nancy. "Why don't you start without me and I'll play when we've finished dancing?"

I thought this was pretty tactful, but Nancy didn't go away. She didn't even move an inch. She just stood there staring at me. I could tell from the way her bottom lip was pushed out that she was about to start crying. It was awful. I didn't know what to do. My social experience didn't include a crying best friend at my own party.

If I stopped dancing and went off to play hide-and-seek (argh!) to make Nancy happy, Samantha would probably think I was hopelessly childish — definitely not material for her crowd. If I kept dancing, Nancy would think I was snubbing her.

Suddenly the matter was taken out of my hands. Samantha grabbed my arm and said, "Come on, Liz. We brought all our make-up tonight. We want to do a make-over on you."

"A what?"

"You know. Like in the magazines. You're the 'before' picture now. When we get done with you, you'll be the 'after' picture — with your beauty potential maxed."

I have to admit I was thrilled at the idea of being made over. Especially since I felt I needed it . . . badly. I turned to Nancy and shrugged as if to say, "Well, what can I do?"

As I was about to let Samantha drag me off, Nancy grabbed my other arm and hissed in my ear, "You're such a jerk, Lizzie. You think they're your friends. Well, they're not!"

This made me mad. I hissed right back at her, "You're just jealous that I'm getting this big break."

"Break to what?" she said.

"Well, into the stratosphere of sixth-grade society, if you must know."

"Stratosphere?" she said. "Well, you can buzz off there in your own spaceship. Alone. I'm going home. It doesn't look like I'll be missed all that much, anyway."

And with that, she grabbed up her sleeping bag and stormed out the front door. Ericka Powell rushed after her.

As soon as they were out the door, Candace said, "Maybe they're playing hide-and-go-away."

Samantha and Jessica cracked up at this. I didn't know what to do. It *was* pretty funny, but it was also making fun of my supposed best friend. So what I did was laugh, but not very hard. When I did, the others seemed to warm up to me, and brought me into the tent so they could do my make-over.

Tanya was still in there, which turned out not to matter. She just sat in the corner, and they just pretended she wasn't there — the way they used to pretend I wasn't there. Tonight though, they polished my nails, put blusher on my cheeks, and then tried three shades of lipstick on me, and a mix of blue and green eyeshadows and black mascara. When they handed me the mirror I thought I looked absolutely gross, but I didn't say so. I said I thought they'd done a great job. Then they did each other and, when we were *all* looking pretty gross, we came out of the tent.

I took Samantha and Jessica and Candace up to my new room, and they really seemed to like it.

They looked at my snowball paperweights, and Candace said it was certainly the largest collection of its kind she had ever seen. I couldn't tell whether there was sarcasm in her voice or not. With Candace it's hard to tell.

Then Samantha asked, looking at the door to my bedroom, "By the way, where's your brother Adam tonight?"

"Yeah," Candace said. "We thought he and his friends would be trying to crash the party."

"Why would they do that?" I said.

"Because that's what's *supposed* to happen at slumber parties," Jessica said to me, in the voice kindergarten teachers use when they're showing little kids how to cut and paste. "The girls start to have the party. Then the boys come around on the lawn outside the windows and sing and shout and make trouble. And the girls get to flirt with them."

"Well, I guess that's not going to happen here tonight because my brother and his friends are all in Detroit for a rock concert. It's just us girls for this party. Why don't we go back downstairs and try to get the others to do something more fun than play hide-and-seek? What do you say?"

"What time do you think Adam will be home from the concert?" Samantha asked.

"Uh . . ." I said, trying to remember. "I don't

think he's coming home at all tonight. I think he's staying at a friend's."

"Oh," Samantha said, then turned to Candace and Jessica and shrugged. Everyone stood around in silence, until Samantha said, "It's getting *awfully* late don't you think?"

"Yeah," Candace said, "*way* past my bedtime."

And then Jessica stretched her arms over her head and made this big, phony yawn.

"You mean you're all ready to go to sleep?" I said. I was surprised. It was barely ten. I thought slumber parties usually went on into the night. But if they were ready now . . .

"Well, all right," I said. "Let's go downstairs and roll out the sleeping bags."

"Actually, I always sleep better in my own bed at home," Samantha said.

"Me, too," Candace said.

"I didn't even tell my mother it was a slumber party," Jessica said. "She's expecting me home any minute."

"You mean you're all leaving?!" I said.

"I think so," Samantha said, giving me a little pat on the head, like she was a teacher dismissing me from class.

"You all just came to kid around with my brother and his friends, didn't you?" I asked, suddenly seeing things clearly.

"Now why would you think that?" Candace said, which made Samantha burst out laughing. The three of them started giggling uncontrollably, draping their arms over each others' shoulders. I just stood there watching. I'd never felt so humiliated in my life. I'd been such a dope. Nancy had been right. This whole party — for which I had passed history and cleaned the house and been nervous for days and spent a week's allowance on chips and soda — the whole thing had just been a crummy scheme of Samantha's to get a chance to flirt with my brother. If there was a medal for Prize Turkey, they could have pinned it on me at that moment.

I was beet-red and beginning to cry. I couldn't stand to stay there being laughed at, so I left the three of them sitting on my bed in my stupid-looking bedroom. I guess they must have let themselves out because I didn't see them again that night. I went into the bathroom and washed my face with cold water, then sat on the edge of the tub for a few minutes, getting myself calmed down. Then I went back downstairs to check on what was left of my party. Polly and Diane were getting ready to go to sleep, and Tanya was still inside the tent, studying her science book with a flashlight.

I realized what a stupid party this had been — and all because of me. I was a rotten hostess. I'd been running after the cool crowd so much I hadn't bothered to pay attention to anyone else. And now it was probably too late. I'd probably hurt all their feelings, too.

But then Tanya saved the day — or night, I guess you'd say. She stuck her head out of the tent and asked if anyone wanted to play Clue.

"Ericka left this," she said, holding out the Clue box.

So we all crawled into the tent and set up the game. At first it was a little awkward. I think the nerds knew I'd invited them because I'd been forced to. But then as we played, we started having fun. They weren't as weird as I'd thought, although Tanya was a really terrible Clue player. She thought Colonel Mustard did it in spite of me showing her the card! Around one in the morning, we went in and made some popcorn in the microwave, and Tayna served her beets, which weren't that bad. Then we all got into the tent and went to sleep.

It was not the greatest night's sleep I've ever had. I was restless with worries about Nancy and about having been such an innocent child as to fall for Samantha's schemes. But eventually I drifted off, and when I woke up, the others were already in the kitchen fixing breakfast with my dad.

At first I felt terror shoot through my chest. Maybe he was trying those stupid clam things out on them. But when I went into the kitchen, everyone was having perfectly normal, ordinary pancakes. I laughed out loud at myself for having been so worried. Nobody looked at me strangely for doing this. There were a few good things about hanging out with the nerds. You could pretty much do anything, and no one looked at you like you were strange.

By the time they left, I felt a little better. Not *enough* better, though. It was like, seeing how much fun we'd had at the end of the party, I could see how the whole party could have been. That is if I hadn't been chasing after Samantha and her friends, who couldn't care less about me. And I'd snubbed my own best friend, too. I couldn't wait to call Nancy and make up. I'd straighten everything out.

I got her mom on the line, though.

"I'm afraid Nancy can't talk to you," she told me.

I thought she meant Nancy was in the shower or something and so I said I'd wait.

"No," she said. "You don't understand, Lizzie. Nancy doesn't want to talk to you. She told me she doesn't feel you two are friends anymore."

I couldn't believe it! Nancy, my best friend for all these years, not my friend anymore.

Diary, what's happened to me? I don't know what I'll do without Nancy.

16

Dear Diary:

I know it's been a while since I wrote. I've just been too sad. I went around in a fog all week. In classes, I could hardly pay attention. All I could think about was what a dope I'd been and how I'd ruined *everything* for myself.

Samantha and her friends were back to ignoring me. Not *one* of them said anything to me about the slumber party. It was as if it hadn't happened. Oh, Samantha did speak to me *once*. On Monday, as I stood in the lunch line looking across the room to where Nancy sat talking and laughing at the table with Ericka, I heard Samantha's voice behind me.

"Hey." (Not "Hey, Liz," or even "Hey, Lizzie.") "Could you grab me a bag of those chips? I want to skip ahead to the end of the line."

And when I reached up and pulled down a package from the clip rack and handed them to her, she didn't even thank me. Samantha's mind was clearly on something else. I watched as she joined

Candace and Jessica at a table by the window. Then I saw that Diane Eastman was also sitting with them. At first I was bewildered by this, but then I remembered that Diane's brother Ted was the star quarterback on the Harbor Point Junior High football team. The rats! They were up to their old tricks, only this time with a new victim.

I saw through them now — now, when it was too late. I didn't know who I was madder at — them, or me. I took my lunch tray and sat against the wall, alone at an empty table. But I felt so choked up, I could hardly eat.

On Monday night I tried calling Nancy again. This time I got her on the line, but it was a short conversation.

My end: "Hi, Nancy? It's Lizzie."

Her end: Click.

On Tuesday, I tried to catch Nancy in person. I sat on the bike rack next to Nancy's bike and waited until she came out. I even rode my own bike to school that morning so the two of us could ride home together, after we'd patched things up.

But Nancy wasn't interested in patching. She glared at me, then unlocked her bike in silence.

"I just want to talk to you," I pleaded.

"And I just want to *not* talk to you," Nancy said

in a cold voice — not at all like her — and then rode off.

I was totally miserable and didn't know what I could do to get out of the mess I'd made. At school, I just sat through classes like a zombie. At home, I mostly stayed up in my room, shutting my door and jamming my desk chair under the knob to keep out interlopers of the sibling variety.

My dad was on the road all week, and Mom had had a wisdom tooth pulled on Tuesday and was walking around in her own misery, with a puffed-up cheek and a pained expression. She didn't have the extra energy to notice that I'd lost my best friend. Nobody seemed to care about me.

Someone *did* notice, though. Gram. On Thursday night, she came and tapped on my door.

"Yes?"

"It's your grandmother. Remember me? It's been quite a while since we've seen each other."

"Oh, well, I'm kind of busy," I called out.

"Well, when you get un-busy, maybe you'd like to come up to my place and try a dark cherry brownie. I've just made a panful."

Dark cherry brownies are my absolute favorite. I have no resistance to them. Within minutes, I was scurrying up the carpeted stairs. I found Gram in her little kitchenette, sitting on one chair, her feet propped on another. She was sipping a mug of tea and reading a thick paperback novel. As she'd promised me, a pan of dark cherry brownies was cooling on the formica tabletop.

"You usually only make these on weekends," I said, as I got a knife from the drawer and began cutting the brownies into neat, even squares. "How come you made some on Thursday night?"

"It was the only way I could think of to lure you out of your cave. I wanted to find out what's got you so down."

"Oh, Gram," I said, sitting down with a sigh. "Here I am, only eleven, and already I've made a mess of my whole life."

Gram nodded, and didn't smile. She never acts like my problems are less important than adult problems. So I found myself spilling out the whole sad, stupid story of the party.

"Sounds like you had one really terrible night," Gram said. "At least it's over."

"The party's over, yeah. But the real problem is me. I want to be cool. I want to be part of the cool crowd, but they don't think much of me and, to be honest, I don't think all that much of them. So why do I want to be friends with girls I don't even like? And why, if I want to stay best friends with Nancy, which I know I do, do I insult her and treat her mean every time I turn around? Am I going crazy?"

"I think you're just in a time of heavy-duty

change," Gram said. "And if you and Nancy are going to make it through this period, you've got to really talk about it. You know what we were saying about Nancy and her dad — how she has to tell him how she *really* feels?"

"Yeah?"

"Well, the same thing applies to you and Nancy. Unless you talk to her about how you feel inside, how the two of you are making these changes at different rates — then you two are always going to be having one fight or another. Talk to her, Lizzie."

"But I've tried," I moaned. "She won't! I've tried calling, catching her at school. Nothing works."

"I think you have to find some time and place where you two are alone and there's the right atmosphere."

I thought about this while I nibbled slowly on a brownie.

"I know," I said finally. "On Sunday mornings, Nancy goes bird-watching in the wildlife preserve. If I could find her there, she wouldn't have her bike to ride off on, and she couldn't hang up."

"And she'd probably be pretty surprised to see you there," Gram said. "That might soften her heart a little."

I nodded. "I *have* been pretty crummy about her bird-watching, always telling her it's a dumb thing to do. Just like I've been about her bike-riding and her game-playing and her tree-climbing. Boy, I've sure been a rotten friend."

"Maybe lately," Gram said, "but you and Nancy have a long history together. And a long future ahead of you. But right now you're hitting different places at different times. You need to find ways to be different but still like each other."

"*If* I can even get her to talk to me at all," I said. "What if she won't?"

"Then we'll go to Plan B."

"What's Plan B?"

"I haven't thought it up yet. My policy on Plan B is to wait until Plan A falls through."

I laughed and gave Gram a hug. Lots of times when I've thought something was impossible, Gram has done just this — turned on a little flashlight and pointed it into the darkness of my problem — and shown me a possible way out.

Like right now. I am still worried, but now I really think that if I can find Nancy on Sunday, I might just have a chance at getting my best friend back.

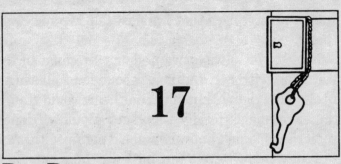

17

Dear **D**iary:

It's Sunday night. A lot happened today.

I got up this morning in a rush to get to the wildlife preserve and find Nancy. It was really cold, so I dressed in a million layers. Jeans and my jean jacket with the flannel lining. My cowboy boots with heavy socks underneath. A scarf and gloves. I was ready to trek around that wildlife preserve for hours looking for Nancy if I had to.

When I got there, I didn't see her bike in the lot. There were a couple of entrances, and she might have left hers at one of the others. But it could be she wasn't there. Maybe she'd thought it was a good morning for staying in bed, and I'd just wind up wandering around the preserve for hours, freezing for no reason.

Still I had to try, and trying meant taking every path until I found her — and I was determined that if she was there, I *would* find her. I'd planned on this search being a drag, but the preserve was such a pretty place that I almost felt happy being there.

Nancy had always wanted me to come bird-watching with her, but it just sounded so boring. I told her I didn't think my poor heart could stand the excitement. Really I am such a pukey friend sometimes I don't know how she'd put up with me.

Today there were a few bird-watchers out, but not many. I asked everybody I ran into if they had seen a tall blonde girl with braces, and finally one old guy said, "You must mean Nancy." He pointed over a little ridge and said he'd seen her there a while before.

I headed that way, and sure enough, there she was, looking through her binoculars, her field guide in her hand — totally absorbed in some little brown bird on a tree branch above her. She didn't even hear me come up beside her.

"Nancy," I said softly.

"Lizzie!" she shouted, forgetting for a minute that she wasn't speaking to me. Then she got really cold again. "What are you doing here? You always thought bird-watching was dumb."

"Well," I said, trying to be funny, "I'm hot on the trail of a purple-and-chartreuse-speckled warbling thrushhatch."

I saw that Nancy really wanted to laugh . . . but she didn't. I waited for her to say something . . . but she didn't.

"I want to apologize for being such a rotten friend at the party," I said, watching her face closely.

I hoped she'd smile, or soften up in some way, but she didn't say anything, so I just kept going. "I want to be best friends with you, but I want to be popular with the others, too," I blurted out.

"Especially some particular others," Nancy said, looking hurt.

"Okay, so I want to be liked by Samantha and her crowd, and I want to *be* like them, even though I don't like them that much. Weird, huh?"

"It's not weird," Nancy said. "It's just *dumb*."

I had to agree. "I think I really want to be this older, more sophisticated version of me. But I don't know what this person would look like. So I'm just imitating Samantha and Candace."

"Poor choice, if you ask me," Nancy said. Her voice was still cold as stone. I worried that I wasn't making the slightest dent in her anger toward me. I tried a different tack.

"Doesn't growing up seem at all exciting to you?"

"No! To me it's just scary. I *know* how to be a kid. I do kid great. But I'm probably going to be a terrible teenager. Weird-looking, and taller than anyone else, and klutzy. I'd like to put it off as long as possible. We *do* still have two years, you know."

I thought about her point of view, and about mine. She was the one to break our thoughtful silence.

"Lizzie. It's just not the same between us now. We're not two peas in a pod anymore."

"Does that mean we can't still be friends?" I asked.

Nancy shrugged. "I don't know. It's harder . . . and I keep getting my feelings hurt when you seem to like Samantha better than me."

"I *don't* like Samantha better than you. I don't like *anyone* better than you."

"Really?" Nancy said.

"Really," I said. I reached over and gave her a giant hug.

"Wait a minute," Nancy said. "I want to be friends but we're going to have to make *lots* of compromises."

"Like what?" I asked suspiciously.

"Well . . . I'd like you to ride your bike to school with me sometimes."

That was a big one. "Okay, sometimes I will," I said finally. "But what kind of compromise will you make for me?"

She thought for a few seconds, then totally surprised me by saying, "I'll try whatever that stuff is you're putting on your lips."

"You like my Lip Enhancer?" I said, amazed.

"I think maybe I should give it a try. Maybe it

will distract people from looking at my braces."

I pulled the tube out of my pocket, and she put some on. It didn't really make much of a difference, but I didn't say anything. I was just so happy she was trying something new.

"You know, best friends are hard to find," Nancy said. "Sometimes you only get one in a lifetime."

It was about then that I started crying. I wish I could have emotional conversations without starting to gush tears. It's so embarrassing. But Nancy didn't seem weirded out about it. She actually started sniffling a little herself.

Then Nancy said she really did want to find this particular kind of sparrow, and would I mind coming along with her? I was so happy just to be friends again I would have gone along if she'd wanted to watch a wall of paint dry.

But surprisingly, bird-watching turned out to be kind of fun. Don't get me wrong. It will never replace roller coasters for excitement, but in a quiet kind of way, it's nice. She has good binoculars, so when you find a bird (she never did find that particular sparrow), you can focus on it and see it up close. And I was amazed at how many birds are hanging out when you get quiet and give them a chance.

We wound up staying in the preserve for a couple of hours, looking for birds, and talking. It was very relaxed — like old times together. I told her I could see why she liked this bird-watching. It was so peaceful.

As we walked along, Nancy said, "You know, I called my dad! I couldn't pretend there was anything wrong with my ankle. So I told him the truth. Well, sort of, anyway. I didn't quite get to the part about my being mad at him. I think I need to work up to that gradually. But I did manage to tell him these weekends are driving me nuts. I told him I thought we should do more quiet things together. You know, so we could relate to each other . . ."

I nodded.

"Well," Nancy said. "It got him thinking that maybe he should take up bird-watching with me."

"Well? What's wrong with that?"

"Oh, nothing," Nancy said, "except he's talking about renting a land rover and getting expedition equipment. And he sent me a book called *Power Birdwatching*!"

This was so awful, but at the same time so funny, that we both burst out laughing and kept on until tears were streaming down our faces.

"I guess you can't change him overnight," I said. "But it sounds like you've made a start."

Nancy nodded and said, "Maybe. I hope so."

* * *

We rode our bikes back together. When we were riding through our neighborhood, we saw Samantha coming out of her house. She was carrying the garbage out to the trash can. The bag was leaking all over her designer jeans, and you could tell she was furious. It was great to see her in this unglamorous moment. Even greater was that she saw that we saw her in such an undignified state. Nancy and I giggled all the way down the block.

"That's one thing I don't think I'll be able to compromise on," Nancy said. "I absolutely hate Samantha."

"Well, I guess I feel pretty mad at her. Maybe we could be our own kind of cool, without hanging out with her and her crowd," I said.

"There you go with that cool stuff again."

"There you go making fun of it again," I answered. We both giggled.

"You know," I said. "I really would like to get back at Samantha for tricking me into having that slumber party. I just don't know what to do."

Nancy smiled her sly smile. "I'm sure we could think of something, if we *really* tried."

"I'm sure, too," I said, and grinned.

It was a super afternoon for Nancy and me. Better than any we had had in a long time. I know we have problems and stuff, but I have high hopes that things will work out . . . maybe.

Anyway, I look at all the blank white pages ahead and wonder what else is going to happen to me in the next months that I'm going to have to tell you about. I hope it's all wonderful . . . or at least part wonderful.

Oh, I know one wonderful thing already. Gram and Nancy have promised to help with however many coats of powder blue it takes to cover the lime green paint in my room.

I'll be back soon, Diary. Who knows, by then I might know how Nancy and I are going to get even with Samantha.

When best friends keep secrets from each other, it can lead to all kinds of trouble! Read Dear Diary #2, The Secret.

W·I·N A D·I·A·R·Y!

Enter the Dear Diary GIVEAWAY

100 Winners!

You can have a wonderful place where you can write down all your special memories and secrets, just like Lizzie! Win a beautiful diary with a lock and key to keep all your entries private. You'll treasure it always. All you have to do is enter the Dear Diary Giveaway! Just complete the coupon below and return it by November 30, 1989.

Rules: Entries must be postmarked by November 30, 1989. Winners will be picked at random from all eligible entries received. No purchase necessary. Valid only in the U.S.A. Employees of Scholastic Inc., affiliates, subsidiaries, and their families are not eligible. Void where prohibited. Winners will be notified by mail.

Fill in the coupon below or write the information on a 3″ x 5″ piece of paper and mail to: DEAR DIARY GIVEAWAY, Scholastic Inc., P.O. Box 673, Cooper Station, New York, NY 10276.

- -

Dear Diary Giveaway

Name _____ Age _____

Street _____

City, State, Zip _____

Where did you buy this Dear Diary book?

☐ Bookstore ☐ Drug Store ☐ Supermarket ☐ Other_____
☐ Book Fair ☐ Book Club ☐ Discount Store

DD289

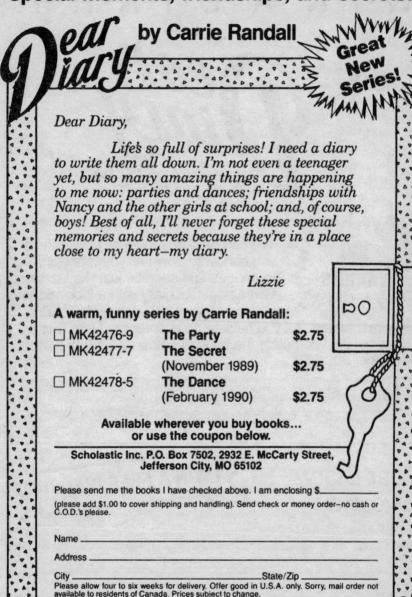

APPLE®PAPERBACKS

More books you'll love, filled with mystery, adventure, friendship, and fun!

NEW APPLE TITLES

☐ 40284-6	**Christina's Ghost** Betty Ren Wright	**$2.50**
☐ 41839-4	**A Ghost in the Window** Betty Ren Wright	**$2.50**
☐ 41794-0	**Katie and Those Boys** Martha Tolles	**$2.50**
☐ 40565-9	**Secret Agents Four** Donald J. Sobol	**$2.50**
☐ 40554-3	**Sixth Grade Sleepover** Eve Bunting	**$2.50**
☐ 40419-9	**When the Dolls Woke** Marjorie Filley Stover	**$2.50**

BEST SELLING APPLE TITLES

☐ 41042-3	**The Dollhouse Murders** Betty Ren Wright	**$2.50**
☐ 42319-3	**The Friendship Pact** Susan Beth Pfeffer	**$2.75**
☐ 40755-4	**Ghosts Beneath Our Feet** Betty Ren Wright	**$2.50**
☐ 40605-1	**Help! I'm a Prisoner in the Library** Eth Clifford	**$2.50**
☐ 40724-4	**Katie's Baby-sitting Job** Martha Tolles	**$2.50**
☐ 40494-6	**The Little Gymnast** Sheila Haigh	**$2.50**
☐ 40283-8	**Me and Katie (The Pest)** Ann M. Martin	**$2.50**
☐ 42316-9	**Nothing's Fair in Fifth Grade** Barthe DeClements	**$2.75**
☐ 40607-8	**Secrets in the Attic** Carol Beach York	**$2.50**
☐ 40180-7	**Sixth Grade Can Really Kill You** Barthe DeClements	**$2.50**
☐ 41118-7	**Tough-luck Karen** Johanna Hurwitz	**$2.50**
☐ 42326-6	**Veronica the Show-off** Nancy K. Robinson	**$2.75**
☐ 42374-6	**Who's Reading Darci's Diary?** Martha Tolles	**$2.75**

Available wherever you buy books...or use the coupon below.